School Friends

Secrets, hopes and dreams...
School friends are for ever!

Collect the whole **School Friends** series:

Party at Silver Spires
Dancer at Silver Spires

Dreams at Silver Spires
Magic at Silver Spires
Success at Silver Spires
Mystery at Silver Spires

...all featuring the Emerald dorm girls

First Term at Silver Spires
Drama at Silver Spires

Rivalry at Silver Spires
Princess at Silver Spires
Secrets at Silver Spires
Star of Silver Spires

...all featuring the Amethyst dorm girls

Want to know more about **School Friends**?
Check out
www.silverspiresschool.co.uk

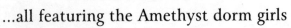

Party
at
Silver
Spires

Ann Bryant

USBORNE

For Fiona Hodgson.
Thank you for your friendship, and for loving my books!

First published in the UK in 2010 by Usborne Publishing Ltd.,
Usborne House, 83-85 Saffron Hill, London EC1N 8RT, England.
www.usborne.com

Cover illustration by Rui Ricardo for folioart.co.uk

JFMAMJJASON /09 95195 ISBN 9780746098646
Printed in Reading, Berkshire, UK.

Chapter One

My name's Nicole Williamson and today is the very first day of my new life at Silver Spires Boarding School for Girls. I can't believe I'm here at last after all the days and weeks and months of waiting. I've actually only been here about two hours, but everything is just as brilliant as I'd hoped and dreamed it would be.

There are six of us in this enormous bedroom, or dormitory as it's actually called, and we are all sitting cross-legged on our beds, talking across the room to each other. When I look at my duvet cover I can imagine for a moment that I'm still at home, as we've all brought our own duvet covers with us, but then when my eyes travel round the room I feel a million miles away from home because everything else is so different.

The dormitory is completely square with a lovely green carpet, and the walls are painted in a colour that I would describe as apple white. My dad's a painter and decorator, so I know lots of different paint shades, as I've seen them on colour charts and in brochures and things. There are two big windows, with curtains that are patterned in dark green and white splodges and go right down to the floor. I think all the green in here is because the Year Seven dormitories in all six boarding houses are named after precious stones, and ours is called Emerald, which is a beautiful green stone. The light seems to stream through the windows, which makes it really bright and I love the way it all feels so modern and luxurious. I've never ever stayed in such a beautiful room before.

I must stop thinking that I'm *staying* here like a visitor, though, because I'm actually *living* here, and that feels so exciting – but also scary, as I'm not used to it yet.

Each of us six has our own big piece of furniture that consists of a desk for our laptops and things, some drawers, a narrow wardrobe, and a ladder that you have to climb up to get to the bed. There are two little lamps – one built into the desk area and one in the headboard so we can read in bed until lights out at half past nine.

Actually, at the moment only five of the six of us are sitting on our beds chatting. The sixth girl, Antonia, who comes from Italy, is sorting through her photos and not really joining in the conversation. She's very pretty, with masses of curly black hair and lovely olive skin. I feel a bit sorry for her, as I think she's only not saying much because her English isn't very good. And I wonder if she really understands what the rest of us are saying. We keep trying to draw her in by chatting about Italy, but she stays quiet, and I'm starting to wonder whether she's just naturally a quiet type of person.

"Have *you* ever been to Italy, Nicole?" Sasha asked me just then, giving me a lovely warm smile. The first thing that struck me about Sasha was how still and calm her face is, with a really open, friendly expression.

I shook my head, because the only country I've ever been to is France. "I went to Paris on a school trip last year though. It was totally brilliant!" I said, speaking quickly, as a picture of the Eiffel Tower and the excitement I'd felt when I first set eyes on it came flooding into my mind. Then I realized that I probably sounded a bit overexcited, like someone who wasn't used to going abroad on holiday, and although that was true, I didn't want anyone to know. I felt sure the others would have visited all sorts of foreign places, and it was important that I didn't come across as different from them. I'd drummed that into myself so often, because I was determined to fit in properly here. Silver Spires is my big, *big* chance to prove myself. And so I gave myself a little telling-off, which turned, inside my head, into a teacher's comment on a report – *Nicole must try to think before opening her mouth.*

Sasha smiled at me. "I agree, Paris is lovely! Did you do a boat trip on the River Seine?"

I shook my head. "We didn't have time. Did you?"

Sasha nodded and her eyes danced. "But I liked the little canals in Venice better. We went on a gondola there. It was amazing!"

I glanced at Antonia, wondering whether she might have something to say about Venice, but she still stayed silent. Poor Antonia. Perhaps she was feeling homesick. She'd had much further to come than any of the rest of us, after all. She was taking photos out of a dark brown shiny box with gold edging, and sorting them into piles. She'd already stuck one or two on the pinboard above her bed. A wisp of worry flitted through me then, because Antonia's gleaming box was just as expensive-looking as her suitcases. I'd seen her arriving at school when my parents were driving away, and I'd had to stop myself from staring as, one after another, her smart suitcases had been taken out of the amazingly long, luxurious-looking car.

Of course, I'd instantly worried that I hadn't brought anywhere near enough clothes and stuff to school with me in my two big, squidgy bags. But then I didn't have any more clothes to bring. Thank goodness Mr. Monk, the caretaker for our boarding house, had taken most of our cases and bags down to the storeroom. Having them all in here earlier had made me feel a bit uncomfortable, because I couldn't help noticing that mine were definitely the scruffiest. I'd felt a bit sorry for Mr. Monk when I'd realized that, because they didn't have any wheels like everyone else's cases, he'd have to carry mine along the corridors as well as down the stairs. I'd even offered to help him, but he'd chuckled and said, "No, love, you're all right! Unless you're here for a job as Forest Ash porter!" I knew I'd said the wrong thing, and I felt embarrassed, but I liked Mr. Monk instantly.

I also loved our boarding house, Forest Ash, straight away. All the boarding houses are named after trees and I thought Forest Ash sounded the most interesting and magicky. From one of our dormitory windows we can see the forest of ash trees in the distance. I'd read all about our boarding house name at home and learned that ash wood is very hard and is used to make charcoal. And in the old days, the charcoal burners would have actually lived in the forest and chopped the trees down themselves and burned the wood to make the charcoal in a special pit dug in the ground. I could just imagine that.

"Which part of Italy do you come from, Antonia?" Izzy suddenly asked, in a bright, clear voice. Everything about Izzy is bright. She moves so quickly and gracefully, like a gazelle.

"Milan," Antonia replied, with a dreamy faraway look in her eyes. She'd pronounced it the Italian way, *Mee-lon,* but she repeated it with an English accent. Then she sighed, and looked as though she was about to say something else but had changed her mind. And next thing, she was straight back to her photo sorting.

I saw Izzy bite her lip and look down, and I guessed she felt sorry for Antonia like I did. But a moment later I wanted to giggle, because the girl called Emily, who I thought might turn out to be the craziest in our dormitory, suddenly flopped back on her bed and said in her lovely Irish accent, "There's sooooo much we've got to get used to, isn't there?"

It wasn't just me who found her funny, because everyone, apart from Antonia, burst out laughing at the way Emily had sounded so dramatic. That made her sit bolt upright again, wide-eyed and palms turned up. Then she deliberately went a bit cross-eyed. "What?" she said, pretending to be indignant. "What's so funny?"

I couldn't help noticing that, even though she started flicking her head from side to side to look at us all individually, her hair seemed to stay completely still. It was the thickest mass of red hair I'd ever seen, and she'd tied it back into a rough sort of ponytail, but there was just as much hair out of the ponytail as in.

It was Bryony who answered Emily. She scrambled down her own ladder and up Emily's, then sat down cross-legged beside her, wearing a big grin. "It's the way you said it like it's going to be really painful

11

getting used to everything! But I think it's going to be great!"

"So do I!" I said, feeling another burst of happiness fizzling around inside me. But the happiness was all mixed up with flutters of nervousness because, although I felt sure I'd love Silver Spires school, I also knew it was going to be incredibly different from everything I'd been used to before. And not just because of it being a boarding school. The big worry for me was that all the girls here seemed so different somehow too.

Emily had already explained that her parents ran a farm in southern Ireland, with twelve fields full of cows, and outbuildings and stables and paddocks, so they must own masses of land. And Sasha had got photos on her laptop as her screen saver, and one of them turned out to be her house. I couldn't believe how enormous and grand it looked, with beautiful tiles all down the top half, and the bottom part painted gleaming white.

"Thees ees my house," Antonia suddenly said, as she pinned another photo on her noticeboard.

I think we were all so surprised that she'd volunteered something which wasn't just an answer to one of our questions, that we jumped down from our beds and crowded round her desk instantly to look at the photo. My nervousness grew as I moved up next to Izzy, dreading seeing a palace or something. But I actually got a nice shock, because the house was only a small chalet. I admit it wasn't as small as our terraced house back home, but it was still small compared to Sasha's mansion. It was on its own at the foot of a mountain covered in snow, and there were lovely fir trees lined up behind it. In front of the main door to the house stood a man and woman.

"Who are those people, Antonia?" asked Bryony.

"Nonna Maria and Nonno Paulo," said Antonia slowly, as though she loved saying their names out loud.

"What's Nonno?" I asked her without thinking. Then I felt my cheeks going pink in case it was something amazingly obvious that everyone knew.

"Nonno ees grandfather," Antonia said rolling the *r*.

"And Nonna is granny!" I finished off, desperate to show that I wasn't stupid as well as knowing no Italian.

"Oh, grandma, right!" said Bryony. And I'm sure she wasn't meaning to correct me, but I felt my cheeks turning pink. Of course it's *grandma*, not *granny*. *Think, Nicole. Just think before you speak.*

I couldn't believe I'd already made a mistake, because when I'd first found out for sure that I'd be coming here to Silver Spires, I told myself that it was really important that I act just like all the other girls so that people would like me. It wasn't that I wanted to be particularly popular, it was just all part of fitting in properly. And I knew from my primary school that if there was anything at all different about you, you got teased or mocked, like the boy in my class who was no good at sport and the girl in Year Five who had a lisp. There were other children like that too, and I always tried to be nice to them. But the trouble was, if the king kids, as we called them – the kids who ruled the class and the playground – saw you being nice to one of the losers, as they called them, then that made you a loser too.

"It's a lovely house, Antonia," I quickly said.

"Eet ees our holiday home."

I swallowed and felt small and anxious again, especially when Bryony asked where it was and then said in a matter-of-fact voice that her second home was in France, and Izzy joined in too, saying she had a holiday home in Spain.

"Well, *we* haven't got a holiday home," said Sasha, going back to her own bed. A nice little wave of relief came over me, until she added, "But Dad's got a flat in London for when he works late."

I was dreading anyone asking me about our tiny house, so it was a relief when Izzy changed the subject.

"Hey, Nicole, your hair's really long, isn't it?" She was standing shoulder to shoulder with me. "Look," she said, clutching the ends of her own hair and of mine. "Yours is at least four centimetres longer than mine. Does it grow quickly, or have you been growing it for ages?"

"It does grow quite quickly," I said, feeling safe in this conversation, "but I wish it was blonde or... anything but mousy really."

"Well, watch out, you two, you've got competition from over here," said Bryony, tugging on a clump of her own really short, dark, spiky hair.

That made us all laugh again. Then, as we each climbed the ladder back up to our own beds, I had a lovely feeling of excitement, because I'd just noticed through the dormitory window that the sun had come out from behind a cloud, and a picture of the main school building with its sparkling silver spires had come into my mind.

The main building is what I remember most from when I came to my interview last term. It's very old indeed, and Ms. Carmichael, the headmistress of the whole school, said it was in a gothic style, which explains the little turrets and diamond-shaped panes of glass in the windows that glint all the time, and the heavy, dark front door with its brass latch. Inside the building there are beams and columns and beautifully carved wood. But it's the outside that I love the best and that's because of the tall thin spires that rise up from the roof. They shine like pure silver when the sun catches them. I can't wait till it's teatime and we go over to the canteen, because then I can see that beautiful building again.

The first time I ever saw it was on the Silver Spires website. When Mum told me I was going to take an exam to see if I was clever enough to get a scholarship to come here, I wanted to see what the school looked like. As soon as I saw the building, even before I'd looked at any other photos, I set my heart on being here. And from that day on, I worked as hard as I could, doing masses of extra reading in the hope that it might help me in the exam. I remember how nervous I was, sitting in a huge hall with loads of other girls, knowing that the only way I'd be able to come here was if I managed to win a scholarship, which meant getting at least eighty-five per cent in the exam. I finished my paper really quickly, and it seemed ages before I saw anyone else putting their pen down, so I kept going over and over my answers and rereading the questions to check I hadn't missed one out or done anything really stupid. And then, finally, the lady at the front told us to finish off, and after that I had two whole weeks to wait to hear whether I would be allowed to come to this dream school.

When the letter finally dropped through our letter box at home, I gave it to my mum to open, because I was just too scared to hear the worst. And before Mum opened it, she looked at me and said, "Nicole, sweetheart, if you haven't got the scholarship, it doesn't matter. We're still very proud of you, because all your teachers wanted you to go for it and they all say that you're amazingly bright." I remember holding my breath and sucking my lips inwards as Mum read through the letter with a frown on her face. Then when she said, "You've done it, Nicole! You've got a scholarship, sweetheart!" I screamed the place down with my *"Yessssss!"* and Mum and I hugged each other and jumped up and down, and my little sisters, Clare and Clemmie, stared at us with pouty faces because they didn't want me to go away to school.

All of this came flooding back to me as I sat on my bed, and it filled me with a rosy *I did it!* feeling as I looked round at my friends, who were still laughing at what Bryony had said about her hair. But then my excitement turned to anxiety, because I didn't really have any right to call them friends yet, and a flurry of fear settled in the pit of my stomach. What if these girls didn't want to be friends with me?

I'd decided before I'd even got here that there was no way I was going to tell anyone about my scholarship. I wasn't sure if there was a rule at Silver Spires that scholarships only went to girls from families who couldn't afford the fees, and I didn't know if I was the only girl to have got a scholarship in Year Seven. All I knew was that I planned to keep the secret of my scholarship to myself, partly because people might think it's geeky to be good at schoolwork and partly because of not wanting anyone to know personal stuff about me yet.

It was a funny feeling chatting away with five people who seemed so different from me, with their big houses and their second homes, and I didn't think I'd ever been in this position before. I'd tried not to stare, but I'd caught a glimpse of some of Antonia's clothes when she'd been unpacking, and they were incredible. It looked like she had to leave half her stuff in one of her cases, because the wardrobes are only narrow. Luckily mine is exactly the right size for what I've brought with me, and the chest of drawers is the right size too, so unpacking was very quick for me.

I'm organized and tidy at home – I've had to be, because I've got such a tiny bedroom. Clare and Clemmie share a bigger one, and they're still going to share even while I'm here at Silver Spires, as neither of them likes being on their own at night-time.

"Do you think it'll be teatime soon?" I asked. We'd come to a silence in our chatter and I wanted to fill it. But my question was never answered because, at that moment, there came a knock at the door.

"Come in," we all said at exactly the same time, and then we burst out laughing. Well, all of us apart from Antonia. She had climbed down the ladder from her bed and was looking at something on her desk. It was impossible to see the expression in her eyes, because her face was hidden by her hair. Looking at it from the side, it seemed to fall in ringlets to her shoulders and really shone in the bright dormitory light.

Miss Callow, our matron, had come in. "And how is Emerald dorm getting on, girls?" she said with a little chuckle. "Making friends? Settling in? Having fun?"

I only met Matron this afternoon when I first arrived here at Forest Ash House. But I liked her straight away because of the way she looked right into my eyes when she was talking to me, as though she really wanted to get to know me. And also, she seems like such a jolly person that I can't imagine her ever being in a bad mood. "You'll be going over to the dining hall for supper in a few minutes," she was saying brightly now, "but first I just want to check that there aren't any more bags for Mr. Monk to pop into the storeroom."

I realized suddenly that I was staring at her, which I knew was really rude of me, but I couldn't help it. I'd got two things wrong. Firstly, I must remember to think of the canteen as a *dining hall*. But more important than that, Matron had mentioned "supper", and, of course, I'd stupidly used the wrong word just before she'd come in. My cheeks flooded with colour again. *It's not called tea at Silver Spires, so get that word out of your head, Nicole!*

The thought of tea sent a little rush of homesickness through me, because I was imagining

20

Mum and Clemmie and Clare sitting around the table in our cosy front room. I wondered whether they'd be talking about me. Mum had decided not to let my sisters come here with her and Dad to drop me off, because she said they'd probably only cry their eyes out half the way home afterwards. They could easily have come along, as it's a Sunday today, but instead they spent the day at Granny and Granddad's. I guessed they'd be home by now, though, having tea and asking Mum loads of questions.

"What about washing hands?" chirped Matron, interrupting my daydream. "All right, Antonia?"

I noticed, as we got down from our beds and made for the door, that Antonia wasn't moving. Matron spoke to her in a slow, loud voice. "We need to wash our hands before supper, Antonia... *Si?*" Then she burst out laughing because she'd managed one little Italian word. I was pleased, because it made Antonia giggle, but it gave me quite a shock when I realized that was the first time I'd seen her smile at all.

"*Si.* I come."

Matron looked delighted to hear Antonia's lilting accent. "Ooh! Do you know, I've been at Silver Spires for many years and I think we might have had a couple of Italian girls in other houses, but not a single one at Forest Ash! I'm very pleased to have you here, Antonia!"

Antonia nodded and gave a small smile, but I wasn't sure if she'd understood everything. I hung back so I could walk with her to the bathroom, as the other four had gone off already. But she looked down and I had the feeling she didn't want to come with me, which hurt me a bit. I quickly told myself not to be silly, and went to catch up with the others.

Just ahead of me, Emily was telling Bryony that she was glad she was in Emerald dorm because she came from the Emerald Isle. Bryony asked Emily what she meant, but I knew from my geography that "the Emerald Isle" is the nickname for Ireland. Just behind them, Sasha had linked arms with Izzy and was trying to imitate Izzy's way of walking with her toes turned out.

"I bet you've done ballet, Izzy, haven't you?"

I didn't hear Izzy's answer though, because the four of them had gone into the bathroom by then.

"Hey, Nicole! Look at the tiles in here!" Bryony poked her head back out of the doorway and was beckoning to me to hurry up. I didn't need telling twice. I rushed to join them.

It was true, the tiles on the walls of the shower

were beautiful. Lots of them were plain white, but every so often there was an odd one with a picture or a colourful pattern on it.

"This is my favourite!" said Emily, pointing to a tile with an orchard on it.

After that, everyone started searching for their favourite tiles, and in the end Matron had to tell us to hurry up and wash our hands. "Mrs. Pridham's going to be after me, wondering what I've done with Emerald dorm!" she said in her hearty voice. Mrs. Pridham is the housemistress of Forest Ash, but it was Miss Stevenson, the assistant housemistress, who appeared. "All the others have set off to supper," she said quietly to Matron.

"There you are! What did I tell you?" Matron chuckled. "We're late! Go on now!"

As we followed Miss Stevenson downstairs, there seemed to be a different feeling in the air, and I wondered whether the others were getting at all nervous, like I was, about what was in store. Probably not. After all, we were only going to have tea – I mean, *supper*. But for me it was a big event. This was where it all began, my new life. I was going to see those beautiful silver spires in a moment, then sit in the canteen – I mean the dining hall – and be just one little Year Seven amongst all those other girls, from eleven-year-olds like me, right up to sixteen-year-olds. At least there wouldn't be any seventeen and eighteen-year-olds there, because the sixth form part of the school is on different premises.

I swallowed and glanced back upstairs at the sound of a mobile bleeping. Antonia was pulling her phone out of her pocket, and I saw her flip it open in a quick one-handed gesture. Turning back round again, I noticed Mrs. Pridham standing at the bottom of the stairs wearing a half smile, as though she wanted us to hurry up but wasn't exactly cross.

"Sorry we're late!" said Emily, grinning. Then she and Bryony were first to go out of the Forest Ash main entrance and I saw Emily throw her arms up dramatically. "Lovely fresh air!" she said, which made Mrs. Pridham and Matron exchange a smile.

I caught up with Sasha and Izzy and the three of us went out together. The other two were taking turns to guess what we might be having for supper. But I was quiet. Any second now we'd turn the corner...

And when we did, I gasped. "Look!"

The others stopped in their tracks and we all stared up at the tall spires. But a moment later they were rushing off again, chatting away. And then Antonia was right beside me.

"Like...what ees the name for them? *Diamanti*," she breathed.

"Yes, diamonds," I whispered. And when I looked at her, I saw that she felt exactly as I did.

Just knowing that made me so happy.

Chapter Two

The moment I walked into the dining hall I knew I'd never again call it a canteen by mistake. It was such a grand and elegant room and, as I took my place in the queue, I found myself imagining a time hundreds of years before when it wouldn't have been part of a school. I could just picture all the ladies in their fine dresses and the gentlemen wearing powdered wigs, and it seemed incredible that they'd trodden these same wooden floorboards that I was treading right now.

"Oh great! Lamb balti!" said Sasha reading out from the menu on the blackboard as we shuffled forwards.

I didn't know what to say. Mum never cooked things like lamb balti. I didn't know if I was going to like it.

"And apple flan!" said Emily, eyes gleaming. "Let's hope that's with custard."

We six sat at an empty table at one end of the room. The next-door table was full of Year Sevens too, but there were girls of all age groups dotted about over the rest of the hall. I heard the name Hazeldean mentioned at the table beside us, and that got us six into a conversation about the different houses. Well, us five. Antonia was with us, but she still wore her closed expression, and I noticed she only took tiny mouthfuls of food.

"I'm glad our house colour is red," said Emily. "I think red is great, which is lucky for me, as I was born with this mop!"

I liked the way Emily said exactly what she thought, and didn't seem to worry about anything. I wished I could be like that.

"What are the other houses called?" asked Bryony. "I can only remember Hazeldean and Elm-something-or-other."

"Elmhurst," I told her, feeling pleased to be able to answer her question. "Then there's Willowhaven, Oakley and Beech House."

"Oh wow!" said Emily. "Do you know what their colours are?"

Without thinking, I recited them quickly. "Forest Ash is red, Hazeldean's purple, Elmhurst is white, Willowhaven's green, Oakley is yellow and Beech House is blue."

It was only when I realized everyone was looking at me that I worried in case I'd sounded show-offy. It's just always been easy for me to remember lists of things, especially if I'm really interested in the subject. But the last thing I wanted was for anyone to think I was trying to prove how clever I was.

"Bit of a walking encyclopaedia, aren't you, Nicole?" said Emily. She was grinning, but I still felt uncomfortable.

"I...I can only remember certain things... I mean...not everything..." My eyes happened to meet Antonia's at that moment and she looked away abruptly, which made my stomach tighten. She probably hadn't understood a single word I'd said, as I'd reeled the houses and their colours off in such a gabble. I told myself to speak more slowly in future. And I also reminded myself to *think* before I spoke at all.

You're trying to fit in, remember, Nicole.

I was desperate for someone to change the

subject, but when Sasha suddenly looked into the distance, her hand hovering in front of her face with a forkful of food, and said, "I wonder if my mum and dad are missing me..." I forgot all about fitting in, as a little rush of sadness came over me.

My parents have been separated for the last eight months. They used to argue horribly all the time, and it was almost a relief when they split up. We get to see Dad every other weekend now and he phones us at least twice a week. I can tell he's trying to show us that he loves us just as much as ever, even though he's not actually living with us. It's sad without Dad in the house, but at least in one way it's better because there are no more arguments. Unfortunately he and Mum obviously thought I'd want them to be together on the special occasion of dropping me off on my first day here at Silver Spires. And it was true, I did think it was a lovely idea, but I changed my mind roughly halfway through the journey when they started a massive argument about the fact that Dad hadn't cleaned or tidied the car.

Dad said there hadn't been any need to tidy up his cans of paints and his ladders and dust sheets and things that were in the boot, because my two squashy bags easily fitted in. And as for cleaning the car, he said he hadn't had time because he spent every hour trying to earn enough money to pay for Mum and us lot, as well as his own flat. Hearing him sounding so angry had sent me straight back to the time when he lived at home and I used to hear the cross voices coming up through the kitchen ceiling into my room.

I shrank down in the back of the car and Mum spoke in sharp whispers through her teeth, as though that would protect me from the argument. She said it was going to be totally embarrassing arriving at a posh private school in a dirty old Volvo estate and that Dad should have thought about that, and it was typical of him that he hadn't.

The argument kept on coming to an end, or so I thought, but then after a few minutes of silence, or after I'd tried my best to change the conversation, one or other of them would bring it back again with a very final-sounding sentence, as though they were determined to have the last word. It was Dad who managed it. "Well, don't bother to come next time, if you're that ashamed of the car. I'll collect Nicole without you." I'd felt sorry for Mum at that moment, because she didn't have a car of her own yet, though she kept saying it wouldn't be long till she could afford one.

I remember how we'd turned into the long Silver

Spires drive then and found ourselves in a line of the smartest, newest cars I'd ever seen in my life. And Mum hadn't sounded cross then, just really anxious, as she'd pointed out the makes of some of the cars and compared them to our old Volvo.

It had been a relief when my parents had finally gone, because I didn't have to listen to them snapping at each other any more. But in another, bigger way, I'd also felt a heavy sadness weighing me down. I love both my parents and it hurts me when they argue. I'm not going to be seeing them for ages and I didn't like the horrible memory I was left with, that was now running through my head as I sat here in the Silver Spires dining hall, listening to everyone talking around me, and trying to think of the right things to say.

"Well, my parents definitely won't be missing me," Emily said, bringing me back to the present, and then she craned her neck to see what was happening at the counter where the food was being served. "When do you think we can get pudding?"

An older girl from the table behind must have heard her. "You can help yourself whenever you're ready. The puddings are over there, see."

Emily thanked her and got up with her plate. "Dad'll be getting the cows in so Mum can start on the milking right now. They will have forgotten all about little me!" She laughed and I envied her again for taking everything so casually.

"My parents will probably be watching telly with my brother and sister," said Izzy. She sighed. "I expect they're feeling a bit funny without me there."

"Well, my mum will be giving the babies a bath or something," said Sasha, rolling her eyes.

"Babies? Are they twins?" asked Izzy.

Sasha nodded. "And Dad will be on his computer, working away. He doesn't stop working ever. Not even on Sundays."

"What's his job?" asked Bryony.

"He's a company director."

"Oh, snap! My mum's a company director!" said Bryony.

Then a girl from the next table, who must have been tuning into our conversation, suddenly said, "Both my parents are company directors, actually!" She was looking at Bryony as if to say, *So what's the big deal?* And I didn't like the way she'd spoken in a kind of posh drawl, her eyes all cold and clever.

My heart started hammering. Any second now someone would ask about *my* parents' jobs, and how could I admit that Dad's a painter and decorator and Mum works in a supermarket? I looked at Antonia to see if she'd been following the conversation. It would be great if someone thought to ask about her family before they asked about mine. It might turn out that her parents had got such interesting jobs that we wouldn't ever get round to finding out about what my mum and dad did. Or maybe Antonia would have trouble explaining because of her English not being fluent, and we'd take so long trying to understand what she meant that I'd be completely forgotten. I ought to quickly ask her myself, but then if I did that, she might give a one-word answer and ask me straight back.

Quick, change the conversation, Nicole.

But I was too late. Izzy had turned to me.

"What do your parents do, Nicole?"

The girl on the next table had fixed me with her cold gaze. I wished she'd go back to talking to the people on her own table.

"Dad's a…" *I can't say decorator…I just can't say it. Everyone will stare at me. The nasty girl will snigger.* "…a painter."

It wasn't a lie exactly, but I'd deliberately given completely the wrong impression. I hadn't explained to them that it wasn't pictures he painted, but houses.

"My auntie loves to paint too," said Izzy. "She's really arty!"

"Can you pass the water, please, Suki?"

And with that, thank goodness, the girl turned back to her own table and picked up the water jug. So now I knew two things for sure – one, that she was called Suki, and two, that I really didn't like her.

"Wh...what do your parents do?" I asked Antonia a bit shakily, to get the attention away from myself. "For their work?" I quickly added, to help her understand.

"Papa has a *ristorante*," she answered. "A restaurant," she quickly corrected herself. "We eat good food."

There was an awkward silence. It sounded as though Antonia was saying that the Silver Spires food *wasn't* good. She'd certainly left quite a lot on her plate, as though she hadn't really liked it. I was surprised, because the lamb balti had turned out to be one of the nicest meals I'd ever tasted, after all my worrying. But I was sure Antonia hadn't meant the words *We eat good food* to come out sounding like she was criticizing the Silver Spires food, and I didn't want the others to think badly of her. I searched around in my mind for something to ask her but, in my hurry, all I could think of was, "Does your dad do takeaways?"

As soon as the words were out of my mouth I regretted them. Antonia wore a puzzled frown.

"Does my father take *what* away?" she asked me quietly.

And that's when there came a loud laugh from the next table and I turned to see Suki looking mockingly in our direction. I know Antonia noticed too, because an expression of sadness mixed with confusion came over her face and she immediately looked down and started writing a text on her phone. I felt completely awful in case she thought I'd deliberately said something she wouldn't understand, just to make people laugh.

"Takeaways are disgusting!" Suki drawled. "I don't know why anyone would eat them."

I felt as though she was expecting me to say something back, but the last thing I wanted to do was to get into a conversation with her. I subtly turned a bit away from her, even though it meant I had to turn my back on Antonia slightly. I hadn't thought Antonia would even notice, she was so into her texting, but I definitely heard her sigh, and I so wished I could explain everything to her. There was no way I could do that now, though, and I just had to hope that her sigh was to do with her texting and not me.

It was a big relief when someone rang a little bell and everyone broke off their conversations to listen. It was the Deputy Head, Mrs. Andrews, who addressed us all, explaining that when we'd finished we were free to go back to our houses, where there would be a guided tour for the Year Sevens followed by a meeting in our common rooms with the house staff.

Suki and the girls at the next table got up to go before us, because we'd arrived later than them. As they all left, I made sure I was talking to Sasha on the other side of me from Antonia, so that I didn't have to say goodbye to Suki, and then I immediately started worrying in case I was in the same class as her for any subjects. I knew there were four classes altogether in Year Seven, and that we'd have most of our lessons in these classes. But we were also going to be put into sets for maths, English and science, so even if I wasn't in the same class as Suki for most of the subjects, we could easily find ourselves together in one of the sets, which would be terrible, as she seemed really mean.

* * *

The sun was starting to go down as we left the dining hall and made our way back to Forest Ash. I looked up at what I guessed was our dormitory window. Sasha followed my gaze.

"Isn't it weird to think that we'll all be sleeping in that room tonight," she said thoughtfully.

"Yes, and even weirder to think that we're going to wake up and walk to school and it'll only take about two minutes," said Izzy.

"Don't talk about that," said Emily. "I'm dreading lessons. I bet I'm in all bottom sets."

"No you won't be!" said Bryony.

"I hope we're all together," said Sasha.

"Also I," said Antonia, looking a bit worried, which made me feel anxious for her again.

"Me too," I quickly agreed, and then wished I hadn't spoken because it sounded as though I was correcting her. "I mean...so do I," I stammered. But then Antonia slowed her step. Perhaps she didn't want to walk with the horrible girl who reeled off house names at a hundred miles an hour, talked about things like takeaways that you didn't understand, turned her back on you and corrected your English. I bit my lip, and felt disappointed and cross with myself for getting so many things wrong.

When we got to Forest Ash, a smiling Mrs. Pridham greeted us in the hall. "Miss Stevenson is going to be the guide for the girls from Emerald dorm, while I'll be showing round the other Year Seven girls from Ruby dorm. And then we'll all meet up in the common room, all right?"

I'd been secretly hoping that Mrs. Pridham might be our guide, because Miss Stevenson seemed a bit stern even though I guessed she was only in her early twenties. She didn't smile as much as Mrs. Pridham, and nowhere near as much as lovely Matron.

Forest Ash turned out to be miles bigger than I thought. There are the two big dormitories, or dorms as I'm going to call them from now on, for the Year Sevens. Then there are three slightly smaller ones for the Year Eights, with four girls in each, four for the Year Nines with three girls in each, six for the Year Tens with two girls in each, and the Year Elevens have a single room each. I love the way it's organized. It seems so fair, and I suddenly realized that one day I'd be a Year Eleven with my own room too. That was such a weird thought.

Miss Stevenson showed us where her room and Matron's room were on the top floor, not far from Emerald dorm, but she didn't open the door to let us have a quick look inside, like she had with the dorms.

"If any of you need anything, you can knock on my door," she said in her quiet voice. "I'm on duty two or three nights every week. You have to look on the rota to see who's on duty, because it changes each week."

When we came to a huge room on the second floor with lots of tables and chairs, I guessed this was where we'd do our homework.

"This is the prep room," said Miss Stevenson. "All the Year Sevens and Eights have one hour's prep each evening. One of the house staff will be supervising, or occasionally a Year Eleven. It'll all be written on the rota."

I didn't know what she was talking about, but none of the others looked confused and I felt a bit embarrassed having to ask what prep was. But then I saw Antonia's blank-looking eyes and realized how much worse it was for her, because Miss Stevenson wasn't even speaking her language. And that gave me the courage to ask.

"Er, 'scuse me, but what exactly *is* prep?"

"Oh sorry," said Miss Stevenson. "I should have said. It just means homework."

"Homework," repeated Antonia in a small voice. And I felt sorry for her again.

It was complicated finding your way around

Forest Ash, but the ground floor corridors seemed nice and warm and busy, with all their corners and turnings. The boot room and one of the kitchens were on this floor, along with a room that had a big table and lots of comfy chairs in it.

"This is the Year Seven 'break-out' room," explained Miss Stevenson, "where you can come to work, or just to be quiet if you want to read in peace or something like that."

After we'd seen the laundry rooms in the basement, we came back up to Mrs. Pridham's flat, and Mrs. Pridham suddenly appeared with her group, and insisted that everyone should see her living room.

"This is where you come if you want to talk about anything, girls. When I'm around I generally leave my door open. You might see Mr. Pridham from time to time, although he works quite long hours, so don't blink or you'll miss him!"

While Mrs. Pridham's group went off to see the rest of the ground floor, we went to the common room. It was huge and divided into four areas – three cosy areas, with squidgy chairs and beanbags and sofas and a TV with a DVD player, and a fourth area with a table and chairs – so it was almost like four separate rooms. Emily and Bryony both made for a big beanbag and flopped back on it together. Sasha and Izzy sat in chairs and I sat on a sofa. Antonia could easily have sat down next to me, but instead she perched on the arm of Sasha's chair, and when the girls from Mrs. Pridham's group came in, chattering and laughing, they filled up the rest of the sofa and the other beanbags.

"Well, I hope you feel as though you're getting to know the layout of Forest Ash," said Mrs. Pridham, smiling, when we'd quietened down, "and more importantly I hope you'll soon start to find it's like a home from home! There's so much to get used to at Silver Spires, isn't there? But don't worry, it won't be long before you'll feel as though you've been here for years! Now, I always reckon it takes about two weeks to settle in to the timetable and the rules, and that's when I like to hold a party for all the girls here at Forest Ash." She beamed round and even Miss Stevenson smiled.

Why did my heart start to beat faster?

"So, a week on Saturday, we're having a getting-to-know-you party, when this common room will be transformed with all sorts of decorations. There'll be games and delicious food, some of it made by Forest Ash girls, and best of all, you can dress right up in your favourite party outfits!"

Everyone broke into clapping and cheering at Mrs. Pridham's words. And I joined in. But inside I was panicking. I didn't have any party outfits. Nothing in my wardrobe was even the least bit partyish. I didn't realize we'd need those kind of clothes. And even if I had realized, I wouldn't have had anything special enough to bring. I was going to stand out for being the least dressed-up person at Forest Ash. What was I going to wear? What was I going to *do*?

Chapter Three

The paper in front of me looked neat and tidy. I'd just finished checking my answers for the seventeenth time, so I stared around, and as I looked, I thought what a lot had happened since I'd first come across this prep room the day before.

Today had been such an exciting day, right from the very moment I'd woken up to hear Emily telling us all to "rise and shine". She was in her jamas, leaning out of the window and taking deep breaths.

"Shut it! It's freezing!" wailed Bryony.

"You're joking! It's stifling in here," said Emily. "I'm going for a walk." And she'd got dressed and showered in no time at all, then we didn't see her till breakfast.

The rest of us had taken our time and hardly said anything. I think we were all feeling a bit nervous, wondering what the day held for us.

And now it's eight twenty-five in the evening, and in five minutes' time prep will finish, and then I'm going to e-mail home.

I quickly checked my work one last time, but I wasn't really concentrating. I was thinking back to all the different lessons we'd had. I'd enjoyed every single one of them, and it had been a big relief to find that I was in a class with everyone else from Emerald dorm, but an even bigger relief to find that Suki wasn't in the same class as us. We've not been put in our sets yet for maths, English and science, so I might find she's in the same set as me for one or more of those subjects, but at least I didn't have to put up with her loud voice and cold eyes today.

"Right, girls," came Mrs. Pridham's voice, breaking the silence, and startling one or two people who were deep into their work. "That's it! You're free for half an hour now till bedtime, but remember the rule about not leaving the Forest Ash premises."

"You mean we can't even go outside at all?" asked Emily, and I realized again how much of an outdoor life Emily must have always lived. She didn't like being cooped up inside at all.

"If you want to go and get some fresh air for five minutes, Emily, that's fine," said Mrs. Pridham. "But only five minutes, mind, and take someone with you now it's dark."

"I'll come with you," said Bryony straight away.

"I'm going to the internet room to e-mail my parents," I said to the others.

"Also I," said Antonia. Then she shot me a quick look. "Me too."

I smiled at her but she wasn't looking, and I so wished she had been because then I could have shown her I hadn't been correcting her when she'd said *Also I* the last time. We walked along the corridor together and I was just wondering how to start a conversation with her when her phone rang, and she stopped in the middle of the corridor and began talking really quickly in Italian. So I went into the internet room on my own and wrote an e-mail to Mum and Dad, sending it to their two separate addresses. Then I wrote a short one to Clemmie and Clare. It only took me about ten minutes altogether and I expected to see Antonia still in the corridor when I left the room, but she wasn't there, so I made my way up to the dorm.

"Nicole, look!" said Sasha as soon as I opened the door. "We're all sorting out our clothes for the party next weekend." I didn't want to look, but Sasha had shut the door behind me and was pulling me over to her bed. Out of the corner of my eye, I noticed Antonia looking through her cupboard.

I climbed Sasha's ladder and saw what she'd laid out. There was a pair of black leggings with buttons down the sides, an amazing-looking crinkly pink and purple dress with a swirly pattern, and a very wide black shiny belt with a huge buckle.

"I haven't decided about my jewellery yet," she said, grinning at me as I got back down the ladder with shaky legs. "What are you going to wear, Nicole?"

"Er...I'm not sure, really... Where are Bryony and Emily?"

"They haven't been in to the dorm at all," said Sasha. "Maybe they went to the common room."

"They must have come back in by now," said Izzy, looking at her watch. "It's nearly time for bed. Do you want to see what *I'm* wearing for the party, Nicole?"

"Well, actually, I'm just going to find Emily and Bryony," I mumbled as I turned to the door. But before I went out I caught a glimpse of what Antonia had hung up on the end of her bed on a hanger, and it was the most stunning outfit I thought I'd ever seen. It was a strappy dress that came in at the waist and had a very full skirt that looked as if it would swirl out when she walked. It was in the most gorgeous dark red and black colours.

My heart sank as I trudged back down to the common room. I still had no idea what I was going to wear. I'd only got plain black trousers, and they weren't even particularly silky or anything. And now that I'd seen Sasha's and Antonia's clothes, my best top just looked really dreary and boring, even though I used to love it. Another problem was that my jewellery consisted of one thin chain necklace and a pair of silver earrings.

Even though I hadn't seen what Izzy was planning on wearing, I guessed it would be something just as amazing as Sasha's and Antonia's outfits. Somehow I couldn't imagine Emily and Bryony wanting to dress up quite so much, but all the same, I wasn't going to risk asking them, because I was scared of finding I was wrong. I suppose it was obvious they'd have something suitable in their wardrobes, because who would dream of coming away to a lovely boarding school like Silver Spires without taking any special party clothes? I was really cross with myself for being so stupid that I hadn't asked Mum for just one dress.

By Wednesday, I found out that I'd been put in top sets for maths, science and English. I was really pleased, because my parents had drummed it into me that I had to keep working hard throughout all my time at Silver Spires, otherwise there was a chance I might have my scholarship taken away. And it was only because of the scholarship that I was at the school in the first place. I remember when we were buying my uniform, Mum kept on biting her lip and frowning as she looked at the prices of the different items, because it all seemed so expensive and we still had the PE kit to buy. Poor Mum. I was determined never to do anything except my total best in lessons, so then I wouldn't risk losing my precious scholarship.

Of the girls in my dorm, I was the only one to be put in all top sets. The others were in a mixture of top, middle and bottom, except for Antonia, who was in all bottom sets. That was only because of her problem with the language though. I'd heard Mrs. Pridham explaining to her that as she got better at English, her teachers would be able to assess her better and she might find she changed sets. In the meantime she would get lots of extra help with her English. And it was true, she was already understanding much more of what we all said. Suki wasn't in the same set as me for anything, thank goodness, so that was one worry I could strike off my list.

And soon I was able to strike off another one. As far as lessons were concerned, I felt as though I was fitting in fine, and I certainly wasn't the only one to be in all top sets. I still didn't want anyone to find out about my scholarship, though, but at least no one thought I was geeky or odd. And then once, when the six of us were in our dorm together, all sitting cross-legged on our beds, Izzy actually said to the others, "Isn't it great that we've got Nicole in Emerald? I'm very proud of your big brain, Nicole!"

"Yes, we've got our own personal factfinder and problem solver!" said Bryony.

I felt a bit embarrassed. "As long as you don't think I'm showing off or anything…" I mumbled.

"No!" they all chorused loudly.

"No way," added Emily.

Then Antonia echoed, "No way," and we all laughed, because it was the first time we'd ever heard her use such an English phrase. I probably laughed the loudest, because I was so happy that she was joining in, especially with a kind of compliment to me. It was difficult to work Antonia out. Most of the time she seemed quite aloof with everyone, but I couldn't help feeling it was *all* of the time that she was aloof with me, and I felt anxious again that we'd got off to a bad start in the dining hall.

Meanwhile, the big problem about what to wear for the party wouldn't go away, although there was one piece of good news that I was clinging to like mad. At lunchtime on Thursday, Sasha suddenly started talking about a shopping trip at the weekend.

"It'll be really cool. We get to go in the school minibuses and we're free to wander round on our own as long as we've got at least one other person with us. I'm going to buy some shoes for the party, because I don't like the ones I've got all that much."

"How do you know about the shopping trip?" I asked.

"Yes, why didn't we know anything about it?" asked Bryony.

"It's on the noticeboard," said Izzy. "But Sash and I also heard some of the Year Eights talking about it in the common room last night. They said there are shopping trips just about every weekend, and the Year Sevens are always desperate to go, but by the time you get to Year Eight, you're not that bothered any more."

"I'd love to go," I said, thinking that this was the perfect solution to my problem. I'd simply buy a new dress or new trousers or a new top. Immediately after I'd had the thought I started to feel guilty, though, because I didn't have all that much spending money and I knew I must make it last for the whole term. Buying clothes on the very first weekend wasn't a good idea. But, really, I had no choice. I'd just have to stay away from all shopping trips for the rest of the term.

"I'm going riding on Saturday," said Emily firmly. "I can't wait. I just wish I could magic my own pony here to Silver Spires."

"Where are the stables?" asked Bryony.

"Haven't a clue. All I know is that Miss Stevenson says there are riding trips every weekend."

"I think I'll spend Saturday afternoon exploring," Bryony said. "Horses and me don't really mix, and neither do shopping and me."

"Will you be all right on your own?" Emily asked her.

"Yes, I quite like being on my own sometimes. I'm going to find out about every inch of this place, including all the other boarding houses – then I can be sure that Forest Ash really is the best!"

We laughed, then Izzy turned to Antonia and spoke slowly. "What about you? Do you want to come on the shopping trip?"

Antonia nodded. "Yes. I like to," she said quietly.

As we carried on eating and chatting, I found myself relaxing. I was really enjoying the halloumi salad. I'd never heard of halloumi cheese before today, but I was definitely going to tell Mum about it so hopefully we could eat it at home sometime. It looked as though it had been cooked, and I was desperate to find out if that's what you're supposed to do with halloumi cheese, but I didn't dare ask in case everyone thought it was pathetic not knowing the answer to such a simple question.

"Thees ees Greek cheese," Antonia suddenly said to no one in particular. "Papa likes all things Italian, but he also likes to cook halloumi, because eet doesn't melt."

I felt happy that my question had been answered just like that and I decided to have another try to get Antonia to be friendly towards me. "It must be great to taste so many delicious foods all the time,"

I said as clearly as I could.

"Yes, I like very much," she replied, looking right at me. She didn't smile or anything, but I was pleased that she'd looked at me properly. Then, just when I thought how well this whole lunch was going, Suki came and sat at our table and my spirits sank. I'd seen her trying to squash in with some Hazeldean girls and I don't think she was very impressed that there wasn't any room and she'd had to sit with the Forest Ash lot.

"What are you talking about?" she asked rather abruptly, as soon as she'd sat down.

"Antonia's restaurant," said Izzy.

"What? You've got a restaurant?" Suki asked in a loud voice, as though Antonia was stupid or deaf.

Antonia nodded. "In Milan."

"In Milan, right. I've been there. What's the restaurant called?"

"Ristorante Alessandro – my papa's name."

"Is your father the manager or the owner?"

It really annoyed me that Suki wanted to know the answer to that question. What difference did it make to her?

"He owns the restaurant."

Suki smiled. "I'll tell my parents. They're often in Milan on business."

Antonia smiled back but she didn't make any comment.

"I love halloumi cheese," went on Suki. "My dad goes to Greece quite often too. That's where it comes from, you know."

"We know," said Emily, a bit snappily.

Suki didn't seem to notice Emily's tone, because she went on, "I had a real craze on anything to do with Greece at one stage. My dad taught me quite a few Greek words."

"Oh, I had to learn the Greek alphabet for school. Alpha, beta, gamma, delta..." spouted Bryony. "That's the first four letters. I can't remember what comes next. Do you know, Suki?"

Suki laughed. "How should I know? People who can recite things like the Greek alphabet and the kings of England and the periodic table of elements are really sad, in my opinion. They ought to get a life!"

I felt my shoulders rising with tension and my face getting hot. I was one of those people who Suki thought was sad, because I could recite the Greek alphabet *and* the kings of England. I just love learning things like that and memorizing them. I know quite a bit of the periodic table too, but not the whole lot. It's really difficult. Thank goodness

I hadn't jumped in with *epsilon, zeta, eta, theta* when Bryony had asked what came after the first four Greek letters.

As soon as I'd wolfed down my pudding I got up to go, because Suki's presence just made me feel uncomfortable, and I went to the break-out room on my own before prep.

The silence in prep is one of my favourite moments of the day. There's hardly ever any silence when you're at a boarding school, apart from in some lessons. You're just surrounded by a buzz the whole time. I don't mind that, because it makes you feel as though you're a real part of something big and exciting. But it's lovely for just five short times a week to be able to bury yourself in silent work for a while. The only trouble is, I always get through my prep really quickly and even when I've checked and checked it, there's often time left over and I get a bit bored. But I don't want to bring a book in, or people might think I'm showing off.

This evening the prep was quite tricky because it was chemistry, and funnily enough, after we'd only just been talking about it, there was a big question about the periodic table. When I finished my own work I happened to glance across at Antonia's. I could see that she'd been given nearly the same prep as mine even though we're in different sets. I noticed she hadn't filled in the grid of the periodic elements at all, and I don't know whether she sensed me looking, but she suddenly turned to me and pointed to her empty grid, then gave a huge shrug, rolling her eyes as if to say, *This is impossible! Don't you agree?*

Before I even knew it, I'd given her the same look, followed by a big smile to show just how much I agreed. I don't know why I did that when I'd actually filled my whole grid in without any problem. I think it was just that I hadn't been expecting Antonia to be smiling at me, and I wanted to make the most of this little moment between us, trying to pretend we had something in common. I shut my book as subtly as I could to make sure Antonia didn't see that I'd actually filled in the whole grid, but she nodded at my closed book and mouthed, "Can you do it?" – her expression changing to an anxious one.

I had to think quickly. Should I show her my work and let her copy it? Or would she wonder then why I'd given her that look as though she and I were in the same boat, when we clearly weren't? Suddenly I could hear Suki's voice loud and clear as though she was sitting right here in the room with us. *People who can recite things like the Greek alphabet and the kings of England and the periodic table of elements are really sad, in my opinion. They ought to get a life!*

I quickly made a decision and mouthed back, "Sorry," to Antonia. Then I gave another friendly smile and a shrug, and got such a warm smile back that I thought at last there was a tiny chance that Antonia and I might become friends. I hoped so, because Sasha and Izzy always seemed to sit next to each other in class and at lunch, and so did Bryony and Emily. It would make sense for Antonia and me to kind of pair up, because I still didn't have a best friend. But in my heart I never really thought that could happen.

When prep finished, the six of us went along to the common room together, discussing the work on the way.

"That question about the periodic table was impossible!" said Emily. "I didn't get what the stupid thing was on about."

"I know," agreed Bryony. "And when are we ever going to need to know about it? I'm not going to be a chemist when I'm older." She stopped and looked at us all. "Anyone round here planning on being a chemist?" Then, before we could answer, "No? Well, there you go!"

"Nicole might," said Izzy. She sighed. "You're so clever, Nicole. I bet you understood that question easily, didn't you?"

"No she deed not understand," said Antonia, with a smile.

I could feel the others looking at me. "No, I didn't... Not really... I mean, I've written something or other, but I'm sure it's all complete rubbish."

Still, I felt their eyes on me, and for the second time since I'd been at Silver Spires, I told myself off.

Chapter Four

I woke up on Saturday morning with mixed feelings. There are always lessons till lunchtime on Saturdays, which I don't mind as the teachers are a bit more relaxed. And today it was the shopping trip after lunch. A part of me felt nervous, because the party was only one week away now and I knew I was about to spend more money than I ought to. But then I told myself to stop worrying. There were sure to be plenty of clothes left in the late summer sale. There were always sales around. I just needed to search for a bargain.

The morning seemed to take ages to get through,

even though I enjoyed all the lessons. We were given our chemistry prep back and I got a hundred per cent, which gave me a lovely feeling in one way and made me desperate to tell Mum, because I knew she'd be really proud of me. But the other half of me felt guilty and anxious, especially as the chemistry teacher made a big thing out of it, announcing it to the whole class, which was really embarrassing. Thank goodness none of the girls in my dorm were in this set for science, and when I had that thought I despised myself for not having told Antonia or the others the truth. But then, if I *had* told them, I couldn't bear the idea that they'd think I'm "sad".

By lunchtime I'd forgotten all about science, as everyone was talking about getting changed for the shopping trip. Sasha, Izzy, Antonia and I all decided to wear jeans, so that was easy. Izzy looked great in her jeans, because she's got lovely slim muscly legs. But when we got changed for shopping and I saw Antonia's jeans, I realized for the first time that there's a big difference between cheap jeans and expensive ones.

"Wow, Antonia!" said Sasha. "I've always wanted a pair of Dolce & Gabbana's."

"I am very lucky, I theenk," said Antonia, not sounding at all show-offy. "Mamma has a friend who works weeth Signor Gabbana. He sometimes gives us jeans."

Izzy, Sasha and I just stared. We were all too stunned to speak.

"Eet ees nearly 'alf past," said Antonia, looking at her watch. "We must go, I theenk."

So we did, in a last-minute flurry of stuffing things into our bags. I hadn't been sure at first if I dared to take my one and only bag with me, because it was a bit grubby. Mum had bought me so many school things, I hadn't dared ask for a new one. My gran had actually knitted it for me in green and blue bobbly wool, and lots of people back home had admired it and my mum called it *fabulously retro*. But taking it on a Silver Spires shopping trip was altogether different. I knew I'd be embarrassed if anyone stared at it.

As we walked towards the main building where the two school minibuses were waiting for us, I saw Antonia eyeing my bag. She looked as though she was about to say something about it to me, but then changed her mind. Her own bag was in soft pink leather with a heavy silver chain strap and a silver heart on the front. It would be no wonder if she thought my little knitted thing was a bit weird.

Izzy and Sasha were first onto the minibus and

they quickly made a dive for the seats at the back, so Antonia and I joined them and I felt glad we were all together. It meant that I didn't have to try and make conversation with Antonia on my own during the journey. I knew I'd never be able to talk about the kinds of things she'd be interested in. It was obvious from all I'd heard about her parents, their restaurant, the people they knew and Antonia's incredible clothes, that her life was as different from my own as it was possible to be.

We got to the town centre after about fifteen minutes and all piled out of the minibuses. Then Miss Fosbrook from Hazeldean, who'd been in the other minibus, gathered us round and told us to listen carefully because she had something important to say. First we had to put her phone number into our phone memories. "Now," she said, "I need to see that you can behave responsibly and sensibly." Then she explained about when and where we'd meet up later, and how we had to make sure we always stayed with at least one other person. "Phone me if you have any problems," she finished with a smile, and added, "And try not to spend too much money. Remember, it's only the first weekend of term!"

I swallowed, knowing that I was just about to do exactly what she'd warned us not to do.

Antonia and I both stayed close to Sasha and Izzy, and the four of us headed straight for Topshop. I suddenly felt very grown-up and independent. It was the first time that it had hit me that Mum and Dad had no idea what I was doing from one day to the next during term time.

Sasha and Izzy raced round Topshop, commenting on everything they liked and didn't like. I went much more slowly, crossing my fingers and hoping that any second I might suddenly come across the perfect outfit for the party, reduced to less than half price. Antonia stayed close by me for the first few minutes, watching what I did carefully. Every time I picked something up and looked at the price tag before putting it down, she waited a moment, then looked at the price tag too. It was quite a relief when she wandered off, but then, when I looked round after I'd been totally absorbed in a rail of tops, I saw that she was standing right by the door, next to a man who looked as though he was completely bored and was just waiting for someone.

It suddenly dawned on me at that moment that as Miss Fosbrook had said we must stay with at least one other person, Antonia and I were kind of partners for each other, although neither of us had actually said that. Sasha and Izzy were definitely in a pair, rushing round together, so that only left me for Antonia, as everyone else seemed to be paired off too.

Oh dear, this was never going to work. It was obvious Antonia wasn't interested in buying clothes from a shop like this if she was used to getting really expensive labels like Dolce & Gabbana for free. And what if we did find the kind of shop she liked? Then I suppose we'd be the opposite way round. I'd be the one waiting by the door – except that I wouldn't. I'd at least pretend to be interested. I suddenly panicked at the thought of that, and wanted Sasha and Izzy to stay with us two. I looked round for them and felt big relief as I spotted them coming down the escalator.

"Have you finished in here, Nicole?" asked Sasha. "Because we have."

"Where's Antonia?" asked Izzy.

"She's over there."

Izzy and Sasha followed my gaze. "Look! She's talking to that man!" spluttered Izzy. "She shouldn't be talking to strangers, should she?"

Izzy was right, and I followed her and Sasha to the door, sighing inside because I had to leave

64

Topshop now, even though I hadn't anywhere near finished my search. Otherwise, the other two might go off and leave Antonia and me stuck trailing around together, which would be terrible.

"Antonia, you shouldn't talk to strangers, you know," Izzy said to her the moment we were out of the shop.

"He was nice. And also friendly," Antonia replied.

"Yes, but you never know..." said Izzy.

"He was like my uncle Stefano."

"All the same..." said Sasha.

"Yes, you are right." Antonia sighed.

"Oh look, Primark!" said Izzy, and my heart leaped at the thought of my favourite shop. There was a strong chance I might be able to afford something from Primark.

So we all rushed towards it. Well, we three rushed and Antonia wandered behind, looking in every single window that we passed. In the end I stopped to wait for her so we wouldn't lose each other.

"After, I would like to go in the bookshop," she said, when she caught me up.

"Yes, I'd like to go in there too," I said. "We can do it straight after this, yes?"

She nodded and I felt suddenly sorry for her.

This whole English world must seem so different to her Italian world and I wondered how I'd be feeling if I'd come to a boarding school in a foreign country and everything was strange. In a way, it was no wonder she'd decided to talk to someone who reminded her of her uncle. I was determined that the moment I'd found something for the party I'd concentrate all my attention on doing the things that Antonia wanted to do.

At first I didn't see anything in Primark that would be suitable, but then when we went upstairs everything looked a bit more glitzy and glam.

I ran my hand along rail after rail and finally stopped when I came to a pink and silver tunic that flared out a bit at the bottom. I remembered Sasha's outfit laid out on her bed, and thought that if I bought a pair of leggings to go with this tunic, it would be perfect for the party.

"That's nice," said Sasha, as I held it up against me. Then she was off looking at shoes at the other end of the shop. Antonia was examining the belts, I noticed. I saw her holding two of them up to compare the lengths and then she frowned at the labels on each for ages.

I looked round the whole shop for some suitable leggings, but none of them seemed fancy enough.

They were all plain, apart from the ones that were thin and more like ordinary tights than leggings. I knew I couldn't afford to go to another shop that was more expensive than this where they might have cooler leggings. And anyway, what if I bought the tunic here and then couldn't find any leggings at all? I sighed a deep sigh as I put the tunic back on the rail. Then I glanced at my watch. There was still plenty of time, though. I mustn't despair yet.

The next shop we went into was much more expensive but it was full of lovely, lovely clothes. Sasha had already bought some totally fashionable shoes and Izzy had bought a bag, and I thought how lucky they were that they didn't seem to have to worry about how much money they spent. Antonia hadn't bought anything, which was no wonder because I guessed she didn't really like anything she'd seen so far. But at least she'd looked as though she was interested in the clothes, studying all the tickets and labels. Maybe she was storing up information so she could tell her mum about English fashion.

For a while she stuck quite close to me as I went from dresses to trousers to tops to skirts, just like she'd done in Topshop. I so loved everything in this amazing shop, and there were masses of things that would be perfect for the party. I knew in my heart though that there was really no way I could afford anything and that I ought to stop looking. In the end, Sasha persuaded me to try on a beautiful dress in shiny dark green material with a strappy top. I'd never worn such a thing in my life and I was excited just at the thought of trying it on. But then I saw the price. I knew it wasn't massively expensive for most people, but for me it was far more than I could afford, and I felt my heart beating faster simply because I hadn't immediately put it back on the rail.

"Just take it to the changing room and try it on," said Sasha. "It doesn't mean you have to buy it."

"And show us what you look like, yeah?" said Izzy.

Antonia was eyeing the dress with a completely straight face. She can't have thought much of it or surely she would have made some sort of comment. I took it into one of the cubicles and pulled it over my head, then smoothed it down and stared at myself in the mirror. I absolutely loved it and it fitted me perfectly. I turned round and admired the back in the mirror and felt bubbles of excitement whooshing up inside me. What if I *did* buy it? It would be all right, wouldn't it? As long as I didn't spend another penny for ages and ages, then it would be fine, surely. The only trouble was that I'd need new shoes, unless my old ones would do. Oh dear. But I quickly got rid of that worry and concentrated on the dress.

I suddenly realized the others would be waiting at the entrance to the changing room, so I plucked up the courage to go back through to the shop so they could see me in the dress. I've only ever done that once. It was before Mum and Dad split up. Mum had come into the changing room with me, but Dad was waiting to see what I looked like too, so I'd stood at the entrance to the changing room, feeling lots of pairs of eyes on me, which was really embarrassing, especially as Dad kept nodding and saying I looked smashing.

Creeping out of the cubicle now made me feel a bit shivery, mainly because I could only see Antonia waiting for me. I looked round for Izzy and Sasha, but they were nowhere to be seen. I wasn't sure what to do then, so I just stood there while Antonia regarded me. She frowned as she looked me up and down, but she didn't speak and I found it unbearable because I sensed other people were staring at me too. I couldn't stand there another second, so I scuttled back into the changing room.

Perhaps I didn't look very nice after all. Antonia obviously didn't think so, otherwise she would have said something. I changed back into my jeans and top and handed the dress to a shop assistant who'd suddenly appeared. Then Sasha and Izzy fell on me.

"We didn't see you!"

"Why didn't you wait for us?"

"Didn't you like it enough?"

I shrugged. "I'm...not really sure."

And Antonia walked alongside, silently as usual, until we'd left the shop. Then she asked, "Where shall we go now?"

Straight across the road was a charity shop. I looked at it longingly. Mum and I often went into charity shops at home and occasionally we found something that happened to be exactly right for me or Clare or Clemmie. There was no way I was going to suggest going into this one, though, except that at that very moment we saw a girl called Sophie from Elmhurst walking out of the shop with a sparkly brooch that she was pinning on her jacket.

"Look what Sophie's got!" I quickly said. "She must have bought it in that shop there. Shall we go in?"

The others all said that would be good, so in we went. Antonia stayed just inside the door looking at the second-hand books, while we three wandered around. I was so hoping there'd be something which just happened to be in my size and was totally suitable for the party, but there was nothing at all and I felt really despondent when we left the shop.

"Let's go back to that other shop, Nicole," said Izzy. "I really want to see what you look like in that dress. Or you could try something else on."

"Or maybe we go into the bookshop now?" said Antonia.

"But Nicole wasn't sure about the dress," said Sasha. "And Izzy and I want to see you in it," she added.

"No, I theenk the dress was...no good..." Antonia said.

Sasha and Izzy looked a bit surprised.

"Oh," said Izzy.

Maybe Italian people were used to saying whatever they thought without considering other people's feelings. But in my heart I thought it was nothing to do with Italians. It was just Antonia. She really didn't seem to like me.

And that hurt.

Chapter Five

I will always remember that first Saturday at Silver Spires as a horrible time. After the shopping trip, I just seemed to sink into a big depression. There wouldn't be another opportunity before the party to go shopping, so I'd just have to wear my black trousers and my boring top. They were the best clothes I had, but they were still nowhere near good enough.

In the evening we went to the common room and watched a DVD with the rest of the Year Sevens, and made ourselves hot drinks in the kitchen. It was a really good film, but my concentration kept disappearing as my mind filled up with worry over and over again. I also felt cross and sad when I thought about our return journey to school. The back seat was taken by the time we four got on, so Sasha and Izzy sat together and Antonia sat down just behind them. There was a spare seat right next to her, but I deliberately didn't take it. I was just too full of emotions to sit beside Antonia, and anyway, I wouldn't have had a clue what to say to her. I sat in front of Izzy and Sasha instead, and stared out of the window at the rainy greyness.

When we went to bed that night, I read for ages, and then I was the last to wake up on Sunday morning. We had breakfast late, and I sat as far away from Antonia as possible. I couldn't tell how she felt about the way I was so obviously avoiding her, because her face is always impossible to read. I wondered if the others had noticed that Antonia and I weren't all that friendly towards each other. None of them had ever said anything to me, but I think I might have caught a look passing between Sasha and Izzy when we were on the minibus.

By Sunday afternoon I'd got myself into a real state about the party, and I was still feeling hurt about Antonia's comment, so it was a relief when we all went swimming and I managed to get rid of some of my hurt feelings by thrashing up and down the pool doing front crawl as fast as I could.

Then Sunday turned to Monday and one really nice thing that happened was that clubs started. There were so many clubs going on every day of the week after school that I didn't know what to choose, but I thought I might try debating club and maybe chess. Emily said she was going to drama, and Bryony was interested in rock climbing in the sports hall and running club down on the athletics track. In the end she persuaded Emily to go with her to running club too. Antonia was excited to find there was a fashion club, so she settled on that and cookery, which was starting that afternoon. Sasha and Izzy opted for gym club and cookery.

At supper time the dining hall seemed to be buzzing with chatter about clubs, and even Antonia smiled a bit and talked about the *ragout* she'd made in cookery. I didn't know how you made it, but of course Sasha and Izzy did because they'd been in the session too, and even Bryony and Emily seemed to know what she was talking about, so I just kept quiet and let the conversation go on around me. I felt a stab of loneliness at that moment, but told myself not to be silly.

After prep we six went to the common room and

74

sat at the table, because Bryony wanted to play the card game Uno from the Forest Ash games store. She spent ages explaining the rules and I thought it sounded like a really good game.

"Thanks for showing me the answer about the continental shelf by the way, Nicole," said Emily as she dealt the cards. "I don't know what I'd do without you to help me in prep," she added.

I assured her I didn't mind and then laughed and said I only hoped it was right. The others all said it was sure to be right because I had such a big brain. I couldn't help feeling embarrassed when they said things like that, but only a bit, because I was used to it now and I was sure it didn't make them like me any less. They seemed to be flattering me, except Antonia, who, as usual, wasn't saying a word. I was still trying to work her out and kept wondering if she was happy in our dorm, she was so silent all the time. I knew it wasn't very nice of me, but once or twice lately I'd actually had the thought that it would be good if she swapped into another dorm so that someone else would join ours. Maybe then I'd find a best friend.

"Right, who's going to keep score?" said Emily.

"Nicole," said Sasha and Izzy at the same time. Then they laughed.

"She's the only one who'll definitely add it up right," said Sasha.

"I don't know about that," I said, laughing. I glanced at Antonia. She was looking through the pack of cards slowly, frowning.

"Here you go," said Bryony, handing me a pencil and paper that someone else must have used as a score sheet.

I turned it over to the blank side and started making a grid, with a column for people's scores and a column for the running totals.

"I don't understand the rules," Antonia suddenly said.

"It's easy," said Emily. "Like Bryony said, you just keep following on with a card of the same colour or the same number, or otherwise you can play a joker...as long as it's the same colour... Oh *you* explain it, Nicole. I'm useless."

The others seemed to fall silent as though they sensed that I might not want to do that, or maybe they sensed that Antonia might not want to hear the rules from me. Whatever it was, one thing was certain – the others really had noticed there was a problem between me and Antonia. And when that fact hit me, a horrible confusion came over me.

"It's...like Emily said," I began hesitantly, avoiding

looking at Antonia, as I picked up the pile of cards and demonstrated what I meant. I slowly explained to her how you had to follow on with the same colour or number, and then I went through the cards that didn't have ordinary numbers on them and tried to be as simple and clear as I could. But she didn't look at me once as I explained, just kept her eyes on the cards the whole time.

"All right, Antonia?" asked Emily when I'd finished. "Do you get it now?"

"I theenk so," came the answer, in an unsure voice.

"How many rounds are we playing?" I asked, going back to my grid.

Izzy looked at her watch. "Er...how many have we got time for?"

"Shall we aim for six, so each of us gets a go at starting first?" I suggested.

"You're so good at getting everything organized, Nicole," said Bryony. "Where did you get that superbrain from? Is it your mum or your dad who's really clever in your family?"

I thought about Mum and Dad and felt confused again. It had never occurred to me that my brain might have come from anywhere in particular. I've just always been the kind of person who likes learning things.

"I...I don't know..."

"You're so lucky, not having to worry about prep and tests and stuff," said Sasha. "I remember how nervous I was when we had to sit the entrance exam to Silver Spires. I know it didn't matter or anything because we'd all got places and it was just to assess what we were like, but I still felt really nervous."

"Yes, me too," said Izzy.

I felt myself blushing. We were getting dangerously near to the topic of scholarships and I didn't like it at all. My secret was still safe, but I wanted it to stay that way, because I still didn't know whether it was only people who couldn't afford the fees who were awarded academic scholarships. I wouldn't be able to bear it when it came to the party if everyone looked at me with pitying eyes in my ordinary black trousers and boring top, and realized that I had nothing to wear because I'm a poor person.

"I'm just going to the loo," I said, feeling suddenly stifled in the common room, scared that my secret might be revealed if I didn't get out straight away. "Start without me. I'll give myself an average score, okay?"

And as I hurried out I heard Emily say, "Average score? That girl thinks of everything. I wouldn't be able to give myself an average score any more than

I'd be able to give myself a back massage."

A big eruption of laughter followed her comment, and I had to admit it was really witty of her. I loved the way Emily came out with things like that. So why was I feeling uncomfortable again? Then it hit me. It was because I'd heard Antonia laughing loudly too. She probably didn't understand what Emily had said but she was just joining in the fun. And I suddenly realized she never did that when I was around. For the first time I had the horrible thought that maybe it was me who stopped her being happy. It was almost as though she was free to be happy now I'd gone. I felt a stab of sadness. I'd wondered whether Antonia ought to swap dorms, but now it seemed like it should be me swapping.

I was still in a state about that as I went back into the common room a couple of minutes later, and my spirits sank even lower when the first sound I heard was Antonia giggling.

"You can't put a yellow eight on a blue four!" Emily was spluttering.

"I know! I do not know why I deed eet!" came Antonia's laughing voice. Then she added, "I 'ave only a joker so I will play eet and you will 'ave to pick up four cards, Bryony!"

"Thanks *very* much, Antonia!" said Bryony,

pretending to be cross, and there was another eruption of laughter.

It took quite a lot of courage to go round the corner and take my place at the table now I'd heard all my dorm mates getting on so well without me, and I hoped and hoped that the laughter and chatter would continue, otherwise I'd know that *I* was the problem.

"How's it going?" I asked as brightly as I could.

But no one answered me because Emily was just slapping her last card down triumphantly. "Out!" she screeched. "I can't believe I've actually won at something! Hallelujah!"

Everyone started adding up their scores and calling them out to me, and for a minute I had to concentrate hard to take them all down correctly and then add them together and divide by six to find the average for myself.

"Okay your turn to deal, Bry," said Emily.

But she'd hardly started dealing when Miss Stevenson appeared with two Year Ten girls.

"Oh no, it's not bedtime already, is it?" asked Emily.

"No, don't panic," said Miss Stevenson. "What's this?" She looked at the cards. "Aha, Uno!"

"I played that last Christmas with my family,"

said one of the Year Tens. "It was hilarious!"

"Do you want to join in?" said Emily.

The girl glanced at my grid. "No, don't worry, that'll ruin your scoring."

"No, it's okay because Nicole can work you out an average score," said Bryony. "She's such a superbrain!"

The other girl glanced at me. "Oh yes, Nicole Williamson. You're one of the scholarship girls, aren't you?"

There was the smallest of silences while my heart thudded horribly and then a Year Eight girl was calling to Miss Stevenson from across the room.

"Can you get this lamp to work, Miss? The switch is really stiff."

I looked down as Miss Stevenson hurried off, the Year Ten girls behind her. Then I heard Izzy draw in her breath slowly. "You got a scholarship, Nicole? Why didn't you tell us?"

"I...I...didn't really think..."

"You brilliant thing!" said Bryony, patting me on the back.

"Well that explains everything!" said Emily.

Sasha's eyes sparkled. "We're sharing a dorm with a scholarship student! Whoa! I can't wait to tell everyone."

Then Antonia spoke. "What ees scholarsheep?"

"It's nothing special really," I said quickly.

"Yes it is. It's when you're so clever that you don't have to pay any school fees!" Emily answered her. "My parents would give anything for a daughter who didn't cost them a bean!"

"Mine too," said Sasha. "I might even have got a bigger allowance if my parents didn't have to pay fees."

I glanced at Antonia and our eyes met for a split second. She wasn't smiling or scowling or anything, but it still made me feel odd because I didn't know what she was thinking. And she never said a word. All of the others had made some kind of comment about my scholarship that showed they were happy for me. But as usual where I was concerned, Antonia had stayed silent. Maybe she hadn't understood. But she must have done. Emily had explained it clearly.

"Actually…I don't really want people knowing about my scholarship. They might think I'm kind of…geeky," I said carefully.

"Oh, you're so modest," said Izzy. "But don't worry, we'll keep quiet about it if that's what you want." She looked round the table at the others. "Won't we?"

They nodded. All except Antonia.

Izzy bit her lip. I could tell she was embarrassed.

"You won't tell anyone about Nicole's scholarship, will you, Antonia?" she said, leaning forwards and speaking slowly, to make sure Antonia had understood.

Antonia gave a small shake of her head, then asked whose turn it was to deal. But we never went back to the game, because one of the Year Eights said something about the party just then, and her comment was like a match that turned a small flare into a big fire, as suddenly everyone was discussing what they were going to wear and how great this common room was going to look when it was decorated. The excitement was infectious. It spread into every nook and cranny, except for the lonely place where I was sitting. I so wanted to look forward to the party too, because I knew it would be brilliant. But I couldn't feel a single shred of happiness about it – only a sickly dread that I wouldn't fit in, with my plain ordinary clothes amongst all the glitz and the glamour.

Chapter Six

On Tuesday after school, everyone from my dorm was going to some club or other and although I hadn't planned on going to one, I didn't want to be on my own, so I thought I might join Bryony and Emily at running club. Being alone would only make my head fill up with sad thoughts, like it had done the night before in bed.

I hadn't been able to sleep for ages because I'd got myself into such a state. My mind had been going over and over conversations and things that had happened since I'd been at Silver Spires, and I'd kept on coming back to my thoughts about being the only girl in my dorm with a scholarship and also that I should swap dorms so Antonia could be happy. Perhaps I ought to go to Mrs. Pridham and ask if there was anyone who wanted to swap with me after half-term? I hated that thought and I actually cried myself to sleep in the end, but they were silent tears so I wouldn't wake the others up.

"Are you going to running club?" I asked Bryony when lessons had finished for the day.

"Yes. Why don't you come too? It'll be good!" she said.

I'd been hoping she'd say something like that and I hurried off to get my stuff from Forest Ash, then joined the others in the changing room.

Two Year Eights were getting changed at the same time as us and started talking about the party on Saturday, which made my stomach churn.

"I think it's going to be even better than last year's, don't you?" said a girl called Zoe. "The Year Tens are in charge of decorating the common room and I heard them talking about an 'Oscar party' theme."

"Oh wow, that'd be so cool," said Zoe's friend, Bec. "I love dressing up. And I think the music will be good too. It's the Year Nines doing that, isn't it?"

My whole stomach seemed to squeeze then, because if it was an Oscar party, I'd just die. I really wouldn't be able to go. It would be practically compulsory to look over-the-top glam for an Oscar party. I could feel my heart banging against my ribs and a part of me was dreading the Year Eight conversation spreading to Emily and Bryony and me, but another part of me was hoping it would, because then at least I'd find out what they were planning on wearing. I looked at them leaning forwards comparing trainers, and realized that there was no way they were about to join in the party conversation. They weren't even listening to what the Year Eights were saying.

"Come on, let's get down to the athletics field," said Emily, when we were all in our tracksuits. And as we jogged off together, I found myself wondering if I dared to ask them outright what they were going to wear for the party. But in the end I couldn't bring myself to do it, because I kept going back to the obvious fact that even though Emily and Bryony weren't the type to dress up, they were bound to have packed *something* suitable and they'd just get on with it because I was sure that it wouldn't be a big deal to them. I wished now that I'd ignored Antonia and gone ahead and bought that lovely dress I'd tried on – then I wouldn't be getting myself into such a state right now.

On Tuesday evening my worst fears came true, because some Year Elevens came round telling everyone that it was definitely going to be an "Oscar Night" party and there would be "Oscar awards" for the best-dressed girl in each year group. Sasha and Izzy immediately got really excited and started comparing jewellery, and then they asked Antonia to show them hers, and she tipped out necklaces and bracelets and earrings all over her blue duvet till it looked like a sea of sparkling jewels. And I shrivelled a bit more inside.

Emily eyed all the jewellery, then said it wasn't really her thing. My heart sang at the sound of those words, but then Sasha whipped out a tiara from one of her drawers and said, "Wear this, Emily! I'll do your hair for you. You'll look fab!"

I was pinning my hopes on Bryony saying something to make me feel better, and when she announced that she'd only got one pair of earrings I felt my spirits lifting.

"Let's see them," said Emily, and Bryony took out a huge pair of shiny silver hearts. "Mum got me these for Christmas. She said they'd go well with my short hair. I haven't even got pierced ears – see. They're magnetic." She put one of them on and looked instantly amazing.

I felt so alone at that moment. Even Bryony, who was really quite a tomboy, was going to be more dressed up than me. If only I was brave enough to ask one of my friends if I could borrow something to wear, or at least borrow some jewellery. But I didn't dare. They'd think I was weird for not having anything suitable of my own.

As soon as no one was paying attention, I slipped out and went down to the internet room. I started to write an angry e-mail to Mum telling her how stupid I felt because she hadn't even thought of getting me something to wear for a posh party. But then I deleted everything I'd written, because it wasn't Mum's fault. She'd probably thought, like I had, that my black trousers and my favourite top would be fine. I tried to write a more newsy e-mail instead, but there was nothing I felt like saying, so instead I went on the Silver Spires website to cheer myself up with some pictures of the glinting spires on the main building. But then I found myself reading the page called *What's Happening This Weekend?* And as soon as I saw the Forest

Ash Oscar Party mentioned, I felt more depressed than ever.

The next morning I woke up feeling sick with panic. There was so much talk about the party at break time that I made sure I went into lunch a bit late on my own. As I stood in the queue, I found myself looking around, hoping there wouldn't be places near anyone from Forest Ash. I just wanted to be certain there was no chance I'd get drawn into a conversation about the party. I could see everyone from my dorm except Bryony sitting at the end of a full table.

But then Bryony came up right behind me.

"What's on the menu?" she asked, peering over my shoulder. "Spag bol. Good. I'm starving."

"There aren't many places left to sit," I said, thinking that this might be an excuse for Bryony and I to sit on our own. But at that very moment two whole tables of girls got up to go so there was suddenly loads of room, and in the end all six of us were sitting together as usual. And then a few other girls joined us, until there was only one place left.

I noticed Suki was about fourth in the queue to get her meal, and I crossed my fingers under the table that she wouldn't come and join us. Whenever she was around, the conversation always seemed to turn into something or other to do with money and how much she'd got compared to other people. And that kind of conversation was almost as bad as talking about the Forest Ash party.

My eyes kept flitting over to the line and willing one of the girls in front of Suki to come and fill the last place at our table, but it was no good. None of them even glanced in our direction. They just went straight off to the other side of the room. I watched Suki take a look around, her chin held high as it always was, then come marching over to the spare place at our table. It was right opposite me. I sighed a big sigh without letting it show, then concentrated on eating my spaghetti.

"Hello, folks!" she said, as she sat down and began poking at her food with her fork, a disgusted look on her face. "I can't stand spag bol like this," she said after a moment. Then she looked at Antonia and smiled. "I bet your father wouldn't allow this in his restaurant!"

Antonia's eyes flew open. "Spaghetti ees very popular in Italy," she said, sounding a bit offended.

"Yes, I know, I'm just saying it's not that great at Silver Spires," Suki explained.

Antonia didn't reply, so Suki carried on. "We're actually paying for this food, and it's hideous," she said, twisting spaghetti round her fork, and using her spoon to hold it in place, then putting it in her mouth and grimacing.

Bryony looked cross. "It's not a five-star restaurant, you know, Suki. And anyway *we're* not paying, are we? It's our parents who pay."

I flinched, and hoped like mad that my friends would remember not to say anything like *Nicole's parents don't have to pay, of course,* but I didn't have to worry, because Suki was carrying on about cooking.

"Does your father do the cooking at home, Antonia? Or do you have a cook?"

"We do not 'ave a cook," Antonia replied. "Sometimes eet ees Papa, sometimes Mamma, sometimes Nonna, or I..."

Suki must have got bored then, because she interrupted by asking the rest of us if we had cooks.

I waited till I heard Sasha and Izzy say no, then I shook my head. Emily and Bryony weren't paying attention. They'd started their own conversation about Emily's farm in Ireland, and I was wishing I could join in, because it sounded really interesting.

But unfortunately they were a bit too far away for that.

"We've mostly got fields for the cows," Emily was saying. "But Mum's got a massive vegetable garden and a little herb garden. I help her with both of them."

"I bet the rest of you have gardeners though, don't you?" said Suki.

I looked down.

"We've got a man who helps in the summer," replied Sasha, "because my parents are always too busy during the week and too tired at the weekends."

"Same here," said Izzy.

"What about you, Antonia?" Suki persisted, as my heart raced and my hackles started to rise. Why was she so obsessed with everyone's wealth?

"Our garden in Milan ees too tiny, but there ees someone who – what ees the word? – *maintains* our holiday home and garden."

Knowing I had to quickly do something to stop Suki turning to me next, I poured myself some water and took a gulp, then pretended it had gone down the wrong way and started coughing.

"Are you all right, Nicole?" asked Izzy, looking concerned. And the others all joined in, checking

I was okay. All apart from Suki, who waited till I'd finished coughing then, just when I thought I was safe from her prying eyes, asked me her horrible question. "Have you got a gardener?"

It crossed my mind that I could easily tell a lie, but Suki had made me angry, and that somehow gave me the confidence to speak out, because why should I care what she thought?

"No, we don't," I said firmly. "In fact we don't have any staff."

I'd surprised myself with my bravery, and I liked the strong feeling it had given me. It didn't last long though, because Suki came straight back with, "Well that's not true for a start, because I saw you arrive on the first day of term and it was a workman who dropped you off in that old car, wasn't it? I saw that the back was full of paints and ladders and stuff."

My cheeks felt as though they were on fire and I reached for my water again with a shaky hand. "This spag bol is boiling!" I said, gulping the water and frantically thinking what to say. The others thought my dad was an artist, not a decorator. "It was my dad actually…he's painting the house at the moment, you see…"

The words sounded weak and pathetic even as I spoke them, and Suki looked at me as though I was talking another language. "Your *dad's* painting the house?"

"Hey, have you seen what's for pudding?" said Emily, coming back into our conversation at the perfect moment. "Banoffee pie. My favourite thing. Well, not the *ban* bit, just the *offee*."

We all laughed.

No, that's not quite true. The others laughed, and I pretended to laugh, and even though I knew I should try to get back that strong feeling I'd had for just a second, I couldn't do it. Inside I was crying.

Chapter Seven

After school on Friday, I went to the main school library. Apart from our dorm, that has to be my favourite room. It's enormous and it's got a certain smell. I think it might be the librarian's perfume, or the furniture polish that's used on the dark heavy tables, or it might be just the shelves and shelves of lovely books. But whatever it is, I really like it. I could spend hours in there, just looking at book after book, because it's even better than our local library at home. And today it was the only place to be. It stopped my spirits sinking right down to rock bottom at the thought of the next day.

I'm not sure which club Emily and Bryony went to after school, but Sasha, Izzy and Antonia said they were going to the dorm to give each other trial makeovers and hairstyles to get ready for the party. I stayed in the library until I was certain they would have gone to supper, and then I took my time walking over to Forest Ash to drop off my school bag.

The Year Sevens are allowed to go to supper any time up to seven o'clock and our dorm are nearly always there right at the beginning. It was twenty to seven by the time I got to Forest Ash, so I was hoping that with any luck there wouldn't be any space left with Izzy and Sasha and the others, and I'd have to sit with people from other boarding houses, and just pretend to my friends that I'd forgotten the time. Then there wouldn't be any danger of the conversation turning to the party. My plan hadn't worked on Wednesday lunchtime, but this time I'd be even later, so surely I'd be all right.

I walked upstairs quickly and opened the door to our dorm. The sight that hit me rooted me to the spot. Sasha, Izzy and Antonia were still there, and the whole dorm seemed to be strewn with hairdryers and hair straighteners and little pots and jars and tubes and bottles of cream and make-up and nail varnish. Sasha's and Izzy's outfits and jewellery were all over their beds. I didn't even get as far as looking at Antonia's bed, as it was the furthest away from the door. I just had to get out.

"Hello, you three!" I said, as brightly as I could. "Hadn't we better go to supper?"

Antonia turned away and started tidying her things.

"Oh, Nicole, you've missed a really cool time, you know!" Sasha said excitedly. "Where did you get to?"

"I...I went to the library. Anyway...I'll see if I can save you places at supper, okay?"

"No, hang on!" said Sasha. "Look at Izzy's hair. Don't you think it's cool?"

I took a proper look at Izzy and told her she looked amazing, because she really did.

"And what about this?" Sasha went on excitedly. "My dress! Ta-da! When those girls told us it was an Oscar theme, I panicked a bit and phoned Mum to ask her to send me something really special, because I'd only got that outfit you saw before!"

She was gabbling away as she slid the dress off the bed and held it up. My eyes nearly popped out of my head when I saw the beautiful dark blue dress, with its silky bodice and full knee-length skirt.

I stared in awe as I took in every little detail. The top of the bodice and the bottom of the skirt each had a little panel of sparkly gems, which looked amazing against the plain blue.

"And these are my shoes..." Sasha went on, smiling happily.

They were very delicate with long lace ties, and they matched the dress exactly.

"You lace these round your ankles like this..." In a flash she'd whipped off one of her trainers and socks and was showing me the shoe. "Do you want to try the other one on, Nicole?"

I shook my head and looked at my watch. "Hadn't we better get going? They're gorgeous, by the way."

"And this is Sasha's bag," Izzy said proudly, as though she'd bought it herself.

It was a small clutch bag with all sorts of beads and gems set all over it. I was trying to imagine why anyone needed a bag when we were only going to be in the common room.

"So your mum sent you the dress?" I asked in a small voice, wondering if it was brand new or whether it had been hanging in Sasha's wardrobe at home.

"Yes! Isn't it cool?" Sasha squeaked.

She hadn't told me what I wanted to know, but,

in any case, I was kicking myself that I hadn't just got on the phone to Mum and asked her to buy me something on her credit card and send it to me.

Yet I knew in my heart that Mum would never be able to afford to splash out like that, so really, when I thought about it, I was glad I hadn't asked her. She probably would have felt embarrassed and gone ahead and bought me something, but then she would have had to deny herself something else, and that wouldn't have been fair.

"Let's see what *you're* going to wear, Nicole!" Izzy suddenly said. "You still haven't shown us."

I felt as though the blood had left my face. "I...I..."

They were all looking at me. Waiting. I had to say something. So I said the first thing that came into my head. "Aha! It's a secret! You'll have to wait and see!" And then I felt as though my insides were caving in and I hardly had the strength to stay standing up, because now I'd made everything a million times worse.

No one seemed to notice that anything was the matter with me though, thank goodness, because Sasha and Izzy had gone back to rushing around clearing away their pots and bottles and hairsprays and things.

But then I was just about to open the door to get away, when Izzy suddenly screeched, "Show Nicole your dress, Antonia!"

"It's really the coolest dress you've ever seen," added Sasha.

"I saw it before," I said turning to the door.

"No, this is another one. Go on, Antonia! Show Nicole!"

"Eet ees too late," said Antonia, shutting her wardrobe door firmly. And when she turned round to face us, I saw something in her eyes that I'd never seen before – something fiery that I didn't understand, but it shocked me.

Izzy and Sasha must have seen it too, because they both looked suddenly embarrassed, and a bit sorry for me. It was obvious to everyone now that Antonia really didn't like me at all. Not even enough to show me her dress.

"Right, I'll see you over there," I said, using every last drop of strength I had to try and pretend that I wasn't at all hurt and that Antonia didn't bother me.

But she did. And so did the party. And so did this dormitory. I had to admit it, I wasn't coping at Silver Spires. I'd never ever felt this low.

* * *

100

Waking up on Saturday morning was horrible, because the memory of the previous evening came flooding in before I'd even opened my eyes. I wished there was no such day as this day.

By lunchtime every girl in Forest Ash was buzzing with excitement about the party and I felt dizzy with the effort of trying to block it out. I could hardly eat a thing, but I didn't want to draw attention to myself, so I tried my hardest to force my lasagne down. The only good thing was that Antonia wasn't there. I knew she'd be here at any moment, of course, but I couldn't help feeling pleased that there wasn't a place on our table. For all I knew, she might have actually come into the dining hall already but chosen to sit on another table away from me, as she despised me so much.

My heart seemed to shrink whenever I had thoughts like this, but I couldn't help them.

"Are you feeling all right, Nicole?" I looked up at the sound of Emily's voice. I'd been miles away, staring down at my food and thinking miserable thoughts. "You've hardly eaten a thing and you look kind of...pale..."

"Yes, you do, actually," said Bryony, putting her hand on my shoulder.

They looked so worried about me that I felt like

bursting into tears, and I was about to assure them brightly that I was fine, when the most brilliant idea burst into my head. This could be the answer to all my problems. I would pretend to be ill. Of course!

"I've got a headache and I just feel...kind of weak..."

"Oh, Nicole! You poor thing!" said Izzy, putting her arm round me. "Shall I pour you some water?"

"Shall we tell Matron?" asked Sasha quietly.

"I can't eat any more," I said in a thin voice.

"Do you want me and Izzy to take you back to Forest Ash," said Sasha, her big eyes full of concern.

"I think I need to go and lie down, but don't worry, I can manage to walk back on my own. I'll just go slowly."

"Are you sure?" asked Izzy.

"Yes, I'll be fine," I said.

"You can ask Matron for some paracetamol," said Bryony.

"And then you can have a nice sleep and wake up on top of the world and ready for a fab party!" said Emily.

"Yes, you don't want to miss the party!" said Izzy, looking suddenly shocked. "Are you sure you'll be okay?" she checked one last time.

I nodded and got up slowly. "Can someone take my plate?"

"I will," came a chorus of voices.

I walked back to Forest Ash feeling a whole mixture of emotions. I was relieved that I was probably going to be able to get out of the party if I kept up my act, but I was upset about the lie. I was touched at the way my friends had been so kind and caring just now, but I was still angry with Antonia for being so rude last night.

When I went into Forest Ash, the first person I saw was Mrs. Pridham.

"Oh, that was a quick lunch, Nicole! You can't have been very hungry."

My heart raced. "I…I'm not feeling well."

Her eyes filled with concern as she put a hand on my shoulder and looked at me carefully. "Oh dear, what is it?"

"My head… And my legs feel weak."

"Oh no! What bad timing!" She smiled at me and squeezed my shoulder. "Matron's actually off duty at the moment, but she'll be back in about an hour and I'll send her along to you. Would you like to have a lie down till then? I think that'd be best."

I nodded.

"Come along then." She steered me towards the stairs, but I didn't want her coming with me. I couldn't keep up the pretence of being ill, and anyway, it made me feel too guilty.

"I'll be okay," I said.

"Well, if you're sure… I should take your shoes off and get right under the duvet – then you'll probably fall asleep, and who knows, you'll hopefully wake up refreshed and ready to party!" She gave me an encouraging smile and I tried to smile back, but I don't think it worked, and I could feel her eyes on me as I started to climb the stairs.

By the time I was outside our dorm I was exhausted with the effort of pretending to be ill just in case Mrs. Pridham was still watching, and I thought how nice it would be to get under the duvet and curl up and see if I could get to sleep. Then I wouldn't have to talk to anyone and I'd even miss out on the party preparations. I didn't really want Matron taking my temperature or anything though, because I knew it would be normal, and then all the house staff would try to chivvy me along and I bet they'd tell me the party would do me good and it would cheer me up and things like that, when they had no idea how wrong they'd be.

I pushed open the dorm door and immediately had a massive shock. Antonia was lying perfectly still on her bed, staring up at the ceiling.

Chapter Eight

A small "*Oh*" sound came out of my mouth.
   She didn't even glance in my direction.

I had no idea what to do or say, especially as I knew that whatever I said she would probably ignore. I wondered if she knew it was me just from my little *oh*. I felt stupid standing completely still, but it would be a bit embarrassing getting under my bedclothes when no words had been spoken between us.

Antonia hadn't moved at all and I suddenly wondered if she was ill. I mean *really* ill. Not pretending, like me. Feeling nervous and unsure of myself, I tiptoed towards her bed, just near enough to see her face. It was streaked with tears. I really couldn't ignore her now. "Antonia..." I tried softly.

She sighed and turned her head towards me, and then I saw that her eyes were full of new tears now and one or two of them were actually rolling down her face.

"Oh... What's the matter? Are...are you okay?"

She shook her head, which made the tears roll across her cheeks, but still she was silent. I bet she was wishing that anyone but me had walked into the dorm at that moment. I felt so sorry for her that I went right up to her bed.

"Aren't you feeling well? Shall I get...someone?"

"I am...unhappy," she said, in the smallest voice.

Me too, I felt like saying.

"Why?" I asked, because I couldn't think what else to say.

"Being here..."

"You miss your family?"

She nodded and her face crumpled and big choky sobs started coming out of her. "I don't...belong... here."

I swallowed and felt a huge cloud of sadness weighing me down. This wasn't what was supposed to be happening. It was almost as though Antonia and I were acting in a film – the film of *Life at Silver Spires* – and Antonia had taken over my part and was saying all my lines and acting like the one who didn't fit in, when clearly that was me. *Wasn't it?*

"Wh...why?" I managed to utter.

"Because I...miss my family...and my home," she stammered in gulps. "And I do not understand Engleesh well...enough...and because...because..."

I wished I could reach up and hold her hand. That might make her feel a bit better, but I was afraid she'd snatch it away.

"...because of you."

"Me!" It was like a punch in the stomach. "You're unhappy because of *me*?"

She nodded, then broke into more loud sobs and hid her face as she shook.

"But...you don't like me...Antonia!"

She was trying to say something, but she was crying so hard I couldn't make out what it was.

"I can't hear you..." I said.

She moved her hands away and I saw that her eyes were all red and her hair was falling over her cheeks and sticking to her tears. "No..." she said through her sobs. "*You* do not...like...*me*."

"Yes I...yes I..." I was going to say, *Yes, I do!* but that wouldn't have been the truth, so I just stopped and bit my lip and felt my throat hurting. It was awful to see Antonia so sad, and something was making my heart bang against my ribs with big alarm.

She suddenly sat up and spoke sharply. "You see! You do *not* like me. I was right. Just because I am not clever like you. Just because I do not understand theengs, you theenk I am stupid."

I gasped. I couldn't believe what I was hearing. How could Antonia have got it so wrong?

"I don't think you're stupid. I've never said that!"

"But you *look* at me and I theenk you theenk I am stupid. And you have a scholarsheep."

My hackles were really rising now. I'd never looked at her in any way at all, because she was never looking at *me* in the first place.

I climbed up the ladder and sat cross-legged on the end of her bed so we were facing each other. Her eyes were wide and protesting and I had the feeling mine might look the same. "It's *you* who doesn't like *me*!" I insisted crossly. "You were the only one who didn't say anything about my scholarship."

"Because I do not like to find you are even more clever than I theenk. And I do not know what is *geeky*. And how can I ask when you do not like me?"

Antonia was being totally unfair and I raised my voice even more so she'd really get it. "Look, the real reason you don't like me is because I don't come from a family with loads of money." The moment I'd said those words, I realized that, even though I'd never really let myself think this thought, it had always been there somewhere in the back of my head: *Antonia knows I'm poor and that's why she doesn't like me.* After that, words poured out of my mouth, each one tumbling faster and louder than the last one. "I don't live in a house in Milan. I don't have a holiday home. I don't have servants. I don't have so many posh clothes that I have to leave half of them in my cases in the storeroom. My mum doesn't know any big fashion designers. My dad doesn't own a smart restaurant..."

"So you make everyone laugh with talking about takeaways because you know I do not understand thees."

I felt a stab of guilt then.

"I was trying to help..."

"Then you turn your back on me."

It was true I'd turned my back, but that was because of Suki. I looked down only for a second, but when I looked back up again I saw that Antonia had stopped crying and her eyes were really blazing.

"How can I know eef you have two houses or eef you have one house when you have never told me? And why should I care eef you have feefty houses or no houses at all."

"You *do* care. It's obvious. You look at me with... with...scorn!" I shouted.

"I do not know what ees *scorn*. I do not even speak Engleesh properly. There ees so much I do not understand but you talk queek queek queek because you are so clever with your scholarsheep, and you do not want to help me in prep!"

"That's not fair. It's not my fault if I talk quickly, and anyway, you never ask me to help you! You never even talk to me at all!"

"I ask in prep how to do the periodeec table and you said eet ees impossible and I was so 'appy that you do not know eet also, and then we take our books back from the teachers, and you leave your book on your desk here and I see that you have done eet all very very well, so you deedn't *want* to help me, deed you? Because you do not like me."

I gulped and looked down. How could I explain what had happened in prep? How could I make Antonia believe that I didn't want to seem too much of a geeky clever clogs, after what Suki had said that lunchtime? It would be difficult enough if Antonia

111

could completely understand English, but she didn't, so I wouldn't know where to start. I wished I'd taken no notice of Suki. She was a horrible girl. And now I felt terrible. I'd no idea Antonia had seen my chemistry book. It was stupid and thoughtless of me to leave it lying around, and even more stupid and thoughtless that I hadn't tried to help her. I could imagine that if the same thing had happened to me, I'd be feeling upset too.

I swallowed and spoke in scarcely more than a whisper. "Sorry...I didn't realize..." It sounded pathetic.

Antonia didn't answer, just stared at me with the saddest eyes I'd ever seen.

"But I honestly thought you hated me," I said in a gentler voice. "I mean, what about when we went shopping?"

"And you deed not want to seet beside me in the bus?"

Now I was cross again. The only reason I didn't want to sit next to her coming back in the minibus was because she'd been so mean to me. The memory of the way she'd silently looked me up and down as I'd stood outside the changing room filled me with a new anger and really wound me up. And what about the time a bit later when she'd wanted to go to the bookshop and she actually said she didn't like the dress I'd tried on? Why was *I* feeling guilty, when she'd acted in such a horrible way? I couldn't help raising my voice again.

"It was obvious you thought it was a rubbish dress that I tried on. You said it was *no good*. Those were your very words! I remember!"

"My Engleesh ees too bad," she said, putting her hand to her cheek and looking alarmed. "I deed not want you to buy thees dress…"

"Why? Just because you have expensive designer dresses, it doesn't mean we can all afford clothes like that!"

"Yes, I know that… I do not speak Engleesh well, so instead of speaking, I *look* and I see you frowning at the prices and I know when someone ees worried…"

"Wh…what do you mean?"

"Eet does not matter."

"Yes, it does matter. What do you mean, you know when someone is worried?"

Her voice went down almost to a whisper. "I theenk you are worried about spending the money, so I try to help you…not to spend eet."

All the thoughts in my mind seemed to be swimming around as though they'd lost their anchor.

I tried my hardest to pin them down. Surely I was right and Antonia was wrong. "But...I needed a dress. I don't have a dress!"

And that was when I realized I'd spilled out the truth by mistake, and the whole awfulness of this conversation was suddenly too much for me to bear and I burst into tears and covered my face.

In a flash I felt Antonia's hand taking one of my hands off my face and she gripped it firmly and prised open my clenched fingers, then held my hand and said something that sounded like "*soo*", in a really gentle voice, and then "*ma no*", and then "*soo*" over and over again, while I cried and cried, two weeks of tears.

"I was...just so...miserable because I thought you hated me," I finally managed to stutter.

"I was also," said Antonia. "I mean, *me too*."

I glanced up at her quickly, because there was something in her voice that seemed to be mocking me. She was smiling, but not unkindly.

"You see, I am even afraid that you have – what ees eet you said? – *scorn,* for my terrible ·Engleesh," she said, her smile turning sad.

I hated that she thought that. "No, no, that's not true at all," I said quickly. "I wasn't correcting you..." I sighed and thought how much misunderstanding

114

had happened between us and how much unravelling there was to be done. "But…but I can see that it must have sounded like I was not being kind," I said carefully. "Only, it just…came out wrongly." Then I sighed again. So much seemed to have come out wrongly for both of us. "How could we have made so many mistakes?" I asked Antonia carefully.

"For me, because I am Italian. But for you, there is no excuse!"

I looked at her sharply, thinking she was cross again, but her eyes were dancing.

"I joke," she said quietly.

"I am joking," I corrected her, feeling a giggle rising to the surface.

And then she began to laugh and so did I. In fact we both fell apart and finished up collapsing into a big hug. Then Antonia pulled away suddenly and grabbed my hands again. "Amiche?" she said.

I looked at her. "What does that mean?"

"It means…are we friends?"

And I nodded hard. "Yes, definitely."

"Good."

I felt so totally happy I could have burst into tears all over again. I'd worked myself up into such a state about Antonia, thinking she really despised me, and all the time she'd been just as miserable about me.

I suddenly put myself in her position and imagined that I'd come over to a strange school in a foreign country and I couldn't even speak the language properly, and this time I really felt her loneliness and then I felt ashamed. My throat was hurting and I knew I was going to cry again.

"Oh no! What ees the matter now?" Antonia asked, leaning forwards.

"It's okay," I stammered. "I just wish...we could turn back the clocks...and start again."

"We can do that, no problem," said Antonia, smiling. She drew lots of anticlockwise circles in the air, then she leaned forwards and shook my hand. "Hello, my name ees Antonia Rossi. I live een Italy. I love my family. I am feeling homeseeck. I am very bad at Engleesh and afraid that I cannot understand or say theengs properly and I am scared that I will not feet een at Silver Spires."

I nodded and took a deep breath. "Hello, my name is Nicole Williamson. I got a scholarship, which is the only reason my family could afford to send me here to Silver Spires. But I don't want people to know that I come from a poor background in case they think I don't belong here. And I don't want people to think I'm a geek or a show-off, either. All I want is to fit in properly at Silver Spires."

"We are the same. We are both worried about feetting een. We weell be good friends," said Antonia simply.

I grinned at her. We *were* the same. I realized that now. This time I was the one who took hold of *her* hand, and I tried to remember the word she'd said. "Ameekay!" I said proudly.

"But are you clever enough to spell eet?" Antonia laughed, grabbing some paper from her desk. She wrote down *Amiche* and I felt surprised.

"It's not pronounced how it's spelled," I said.

"For me eet ees right because eet ees my language," said Antonia. "I will teach you other Italian words eef you want?"

"Oh yes, I'd love to learn some more," I said happily. "And I'll help you with your English until you never have to worry again that you don't understand something!"

"But first, let me show you the dress I have chosen for you for the party."

"You've chosen a dress for me?" Part of me thought I should feel annoyed or embarrassed or upset in some way, but all I felt was a lovely glow of happiness that Antonia had thought of doing something especially for me.

"Of course. Eet ees een my case een the

117

storeroom." She looked a bit embarrassed when she said that, but then we both saw the funny side and cracked up laughing again, and that was how we were when the door opened and in came Sasha, Izzy, Bryony and Emily.

Sasha looked at me with big concern in her eyes. "How are...?" she began in a gentle voice. Then she stopped and stared and I watched the concern turn to confusion. "What's...?"

"Are you...?" Izzy began uncertainly.

I noticed that all four of our friends were looking from Antonia to me and back to Antonia, as though they couldn't believe their eyes.

It was Emily who seemed to take command. She strode forwards. "So," she said, with her hands on her hips like she was our mother, "you two are friends at last! Thank goodness for that!" Then she climbed onto her bed and, just as she'd done on the very first day of term, flopped down as though she was exhausted.

The others looked stunned. There was the smallest of silences and I wondered if they thought that Emily had gone too far. But then one by one, we all six began to crease up with laughter and no one seemed to be able to stop. So it went on and on.

"Help! It's hurting my stomach!" spluttered Bryony.

"And mine!" said Izzy. "And I don't even know what we're laughing about!"

"Neither do I!" said Sasha, setting us all off again.

Antonia and I exchanged a look, and even through her laughter I could see that her eyes were still a bit red from crying, and I expected mine were the same. The others could probably tell we'd both been crying too, and I guessed they might be feeling confused about what on earth had been happening, but I knew that bit by bit we'd try to explain all the misunderstandings to them. And Antonia and I had so much talking to do ourselves. I was sure that she, like me, still had some bad memories stuck in tight knots, and we must take the time to unpick and unravel them together – then we'd really be able to trust each other.

That thought gave me such a good feeling.

Chapter Nine

I was so touched that Antonia had planned to let me borrow one of her dresses for the party. But now I came to think about it properly, it was actually embarrassing too, because I'd given Sasha and Izzy the impression that I'd got something amazing in my wardrobe. I was going to look a bit of a fool coming back from the storeroom with a dress that was obviously Antonia's.

"Right! Time to get ready for the party!" said Sasha.

"You're joking!" said Bryony. "We've got the whole afternoon!"

"And you and I are supposed to be going abseiling!" added Emily, looking at her watch. "Let's get ready, Bry. The minibuses leave in twenty minutes."

"What ees abseiling?" asked Antonia.

"It's jumping down the wall of a high building, attached to a rope," I explained as best I could, feeling happy that it felt so easy to talk to Antonia now.

"Ah!" said Antonia, saying something in Italian that finished with *doppia* and must have been a translation.

Then there was a knock at the door, and in came Matron.

She looked round at the six of us and instantly started chuckling. "Well I was expecting to find an invalid in here, but I must say, you all look in very good health!" Her eyes settled on me. "How are you feeling, Nicole? Did you manage to have a rest?"

"Er...not really..." I said hesitantly, as Antonia and I exchanged a look. We couldn't help giggling a bit. "Sorry, Matron. I can't explain what's funny, but I'm feeling much better now."

"Well I'm delighted to hear it. No need for this then!" She whipped a thermometer out of her pocket, waved it in the air, and popped it away again. "Right, I'll be off, and I'll see you at the party!"

"Yes, bye, Matron. Thank you!" I said.

"You're welcome!" she replied. And on her way out, she winked at Antonia. "Or should I say, *prego*?"

Antonia nodded and grinned, and explained to us that Matron was trying to learn Italian. Then she turned to me. "Let us go down to the common room."

It felt funny but lovely that she was talking just to me, and we said good luck to Emily and Bryony, then went off together.

The moment the door shut behind us, Antonia turned to me with shining eyes. "I do not really want to go to the common room," she explained. "Really, I want to go to the storeroom to find the dress for you!"

I grinned at her. She looked so excited. "But we'll have to go to Mrs. Pridham for the key," I pointed out.

She nodded. "Of course."

So we made our way to Mrs. Pridham's flat and knocked on her door.

Her eyes really flew open when she saw it was the two of us. "Oh!" Then she seemed to recover herself and broke into a nice smile. "Good to see you're much better, Nicole. Did you want to come in for a chat?"

"Er...we wondered if we could borrow the key for the storeroom to get something," I explained.

"Yes, I'm sure that'll be fine, but what about a cup of tea first? I was wanting to talk to both of you actually, but I must admit I'd planned to see you separately."

She raised her eyebrows and I found myself blushing. It was obvious now that Mrs. Pridham knew much more about what went on in her boarding house than I'd thought.

The three of us sat down in her sitting room with mugs of tea and biscuits and talked for a bit about the abseiling trip and other trips that would be happening during the term. It felt like very safe chatter until Mrs. Pridham suddenly put her mug down and looked at us both carefully.

"I'm so pleased to see that you've finally worked through your differences."

Antonia was frowning and I realized she didn't understand what Mrs. Pridham meant.

"Yes, we're...friends now," I said, biting my lip.

"Yes," said Antonia. "*Amiche*."

"That's Italian for friends," I explained to Mrs. Pridham.

She smiled. "It sometimes take a couple of weeks for life to settle down at a boarding school like this, and sometimes a lot longer. I've been aware that you two have had problems, but I wanted to give you time to work things through yourselves before I stepped in."

Antonia was frowning even harder, and that made me realize again how much we take for granted about language. I was determined that from now on I'd help her all I could to improve her English.

"We just had a whole load of misunderstandings," I told Mrs. Pridham carefully.

"My Engleesh ees so bad," Antonia chipped in.

"No, it's not your fault," I quickly said.

"Fault means mistake?" Antonia asked me quietly.

I nodded. "We've both made mistakes. And we've sorted them all out by talking…"

"Yes, we had a truth talk," said Antonia. And I thought that was such a sweet way of describing all that we'd said. "And sometimes we shouted," she added, her eyes twinkling.

"Yes, that's true." I smiled.

"But now we are friends," she finished off, as she nodded firmly at Mrs. Pridham. "*Amiche*."

I felt very touched that she wanted to make this

point so clear, and I think Mrs. Pridham felt moved too, because she blinked a lot and reached for her tea as though she wanted to cover the moment.

"Well, that's really put my mind at rest," she said, smiling at us both once she'd taken a sip and put her mug back down. "Miss Stevenson said it would all come to a head soon, and she was right!"

That gave me quite a shock because I never thought Miss Stevenson would notice anything wrong. "Miss Stevenson?"

But Antonia seemed much more alarmed than me. "Miss Stevenson went to see Ms. Carmichael?" she asked.

"No, no, it's all right," I told her, realizing straight away why she'd got the wrong end of the stick. Poor Antonia must have heard the words *Miss Stevenson* and then the words *come to a head,* and thought that Mrs. Pridham was talking about Ms. Carmichael, because she's the Head of Silver Spires. "It's all right. It's just an expression. If something comes to a head, it's a bit like a spot that gets bigger and bigger and then it pops!"

"Oh!"

Now Antonia looked really bewildered and it wasn't surprising. I hadn't explained it very well at all.

"Do you know, I'd never noticed how often we use expressions like *come to a head*," Mrs. Pridham said. "No wonder you get confused, Antonia. Thank goodness you've got Nicole to help you along."

It was really nice chatting to Mrs. Pridham, and when we'd finished our tea she gave us the key to the storeroom. "What did you say you wanted from down there?"

"Something to wear for the party," answered Antonia.

Mrs. Pridham beamed. "Lovely!"

A few minutes later we were down in the basement, trying to find Antonia's cases amongst the piles and piles of cases and bags and trunks. It didn't take us long, because her luggage all had gold edging that made it stand out, but it was still quite difficult getting her trunk out from underneath the pile of other bags and cases. When she finally managed to open the lid and pull out the dress, I gasped with amazement.

"It's so similar to the one I tried on!" I squeaked.

"Yes. Now you see why I deed not want you to buy that one."

I nodded slowly, feeling a tingling excitement welling up inside me.

"You will be *bellissima*!" said Antonia, beaming. "Very beautiful!"

"Oh thank you, Antonia!" And I hoped she understood from my eyes that I didn't just mean thank you for the compliment, or even thank you for the dress, but just thank you for making everything right for me.

It was quarter to five when we four started to get ready for the party, because Sasha said she absolutely couldn't wait for Emily and Bryony to get back – she wanted to start immediately.

"It weell take such a long time?" asked Antonia, laughing.

"Yes, because I want to do Emily's hair as soon as she gets back, and that will take ages. You see, I'm determined that Emerald dorm will be the best dressed in Forest Ash. And we will!" she added, sticking her chin in the air.

I breathed a sigh of relief that I'd got my gorgeous dress to wear, and to make things even better, lovely Antonia had told everyone that it was *my* dress and we'd been down to the storeroom to get it from my bag. When we were on our own in the bathroom washing our hair later, I told her how kind she was to have said that, but explained that I didn't want her to feel that she had to tell lies to protect me. She wrinkled her nose and said, "Now what do you Engleesh people say? Eet ees a white-coloured lie, I theenk?"

I laughed. "A white lie. Yes, that's right."

"And anyway, I want to geev you the dress, because you look much better than me, wearing eet."

"No, you can't give it to me, Antonia!" I said, feeling shocked, because it was more than my mum would give me even for my birthday or Christmas.

"You want to make me unhappy again?" she asked, tipping her head to one side and pursing her lips dramatically.

"But what would your parents say?"

"They said I must do eet eef eet makes me happy." Antonia shrugged. "Simple, no?"

"You mean you've already asked them?"

"Yes. After we deed the shopping treep. I phoned to tell Mamma that I had learned about Engleesh money and Engleesh sizes. And I also told her I have one dress too many and she was very happy that I give eet to my friend who I theenk has no dresses because her eyes are frightened when there ees talk of dresses and parties."

"Oh, Antonia!" I hugged her tight and felt another twinge of guilt as a memory of how she'd studied all the price tags came to the front of my mind.

Antonia clapped her hands delightedly. "So now the dress ees yours and that means there are no more lies of any colour to tell!"

I laughed as I piled my hair into a towel turban to dry it.

It was five thirty when Emily and Bryony got back from abseiling. They crashed into the dorm and launched into loads of funny and scary stories, all about what an amazing time they'd had. It sounded brilliant and I persuaded Antonia to come with me the next time there was a trip.

"Right, you've got to get ready!" announced Sasha, the moment they stopped to draw breath.

"What, already?" said Bryony, looking at her watch. "It'll take me precisely one minute to get ready, because I'm not going to wash my hair and this is what I'm wearing." She pulled a pair of black trousers out of her bottom drawer, followed by a light blue vest top with *This Is Me* written in dark blue lettering across it, and threw them on her bed. "Plus those earrings I showed you."

I just stood there, my mouth hanging open.

"What's wrong?" said Bryony. "I don't like dressing up and that's all there is to it!"

I quickly shut my mouth and broke into a big smile. "There's nothing wrong. I think you'll look fantastic. I was going to wear black trousers myself, but Antonia persuaded me to put on a dress."

"Show them!" ordered Izzy. "Nicole's going to look so beautiful," she added.

I held the dress against me and felt a second's guilt for not admitting that Antonia had given it to me, but then I remembered how Antonia had stressed that there were no lies of any colour being told, and I made myself let go of the guilt.

While Bryony and Emily were getting ready, I kept thinking about that moment when Bryony had chucked the trousers and top onto her bed, and I felt like breaking out into giggles. If only she'd done that two weeks ago, I needn't have gone through all the agony I'd been through. But of course, thinking back, Bryony and Emily had never really been in on any of the conversations that had taken place about the party. It had always just been the four of us in the dorm whenever we'd discussed what we were going to wear.

Emily put on a pair of dark green trousers with wide bottoms, and a pale green and white fitted cotton shirt. "I don't like dressing up either," she said, "and I told my mum I wasn't going to be seen dead in a dress, so she made me buy these trousers, which aren't so bad I suppose."

"You look fantastic!" I told her. And I really meant it. She'd refused to wear any jewellery, but her hair hung in a wonderful sleek style down to her shoulders, because she'd let Sasha attack it with the hair straighteners and all sorts of glossy products.

"Bit of a change from my usual scruffy self, I must admit!" she said, looking at herself in the mirror, and I could tell from her eyes that she was quite pleased with the end result.

I was also pleased with the way I looked. In fact, that wasn't true. I was actually over the moon. Izzy had styled my hair and I wore it loose, almost down to my waist, with a few thin plaits at the front, which kept it off my face. Antonia and I discovered we had the same size feet and she'd lent me some shoes, and also some matching earrings and a necklace in thin strandy silver.

Sasha and Izzy both looked wonderful in their outfits, and as for Antonia, well I know I'm biased, but she really did take first prize out of us six. It wasn't that her clothes were designer clothes, it was just the way she looked in them. Even Bryony, who isn't interested in fashion one little bit, stared at Antonia for ages, and finally said, "Well if you don't get the Year Seven Oscar for best-dressed person, I'll eat my hat!"

And then we all had to try and explain to Antonia what Bryony meant.

The party was wonderful. The older girls had made the common room look so amazing, with silver spiral decorations hanging everywhere, and hoops that they'd rolled round with tinfoil, and balloons with silver writing. A crisp white tablecloth covered the table and fell down to the floor on all sides. It was covered with scattered hearts and O-for-Oscar shapes. The lights had been turned right down with the dimmer switch, and there were beautiful candles everywhere, and little tea lights on the table amongst the sparkles and the yummy food. The senior students had made an incredible finger buffet, with loads and loads of different scrummy things to eat, and they'd mixed delicious fizzy fruit juices in big glass jugs.

The loud music pulsed through the room, and when I looked around at everyone I felt a warm safe feeling that I was where I was supposed to be. We danced and played games and had quizzes about celebrities, and we talked and talked as we ate and drank to our heart's content. Mrs. Pridham and Matron joined in with the dancing and the quizzes, but Miss Stevenson seemed shyer and stood by herself quite a lot of the time. Antonia and I spent the entire evening glued to each other's sides, and when she won the Year Seven award for best-dressed person, I was the proudest and happiest person in the room.

"I'm so relieved you two made friends just in time," said Emily, "or the rest of us wouldn't have had half such a good time, worrying about you both."

"Have you been worrying about us?" I asked, with another twinge of guilt.

"Course we have! We've spent ages asking each other what to do, and talking to Miss Stevenson about it."

"You talked to Miss Stevenson?" I squeaked.

"She was the one who brought it up," said Bryony, "because she was worrying too, you see, but she told us it was best not to interfere."

"She said she thought you were both too nice not to make friends soon, and we agreed," said Izzy.

"We were really surprised that Miss Stevenson was so easy to talk to," added Sasha, "because she doesn't smile much or anything, but she told us she was quite shy."

"Yes, she even told us she wasn't looking forward to the party very much because she didn't have any posh clothes," said Bryony. "But I assured her that no way would I be wearing posh clothes, and that cheered her up a bit."

So Miss Stevenson had been nervous about the party too! "I'd never have guessed that Miss Stevenson was shy until this evening," I said, thinking how much I was learning today.

"Yes, very shy," said Antonia, nodding. "I can see that."

And yet again I realized how observant Antonia was, which got me wondering what else she'd observed. Had she seen the way I blushed whenever there was any mention of parents? She knew now that I came from a poor background, but I didn't think she had any idea just how very different our families were. In fact I reckoned that if you got every girl in this school and lined them up side by side according to how rich their parents were, I'd be standing on one end of the line and Antonia would be at the other end, with people like Suki.

I kept on telling myself that I was stupid getting scared by thoughts like this. But what if we were just too different to be *amiche*? Now I'd found out what a lovely person Antonia was, I couldn't bear there being any risk at all of losing her.

Chapter Ten

The day after the party I woke up with a lovely sunny feeling and only one little cloud spoiling it. I just couldn't shake away my anxiety that Antonia didn't know the whole truth about me. The problem would be when we got picked up to go home for half-term. Perhaps she'd see our old car and all the paint cans in the back and it would seem so far from what she was used to that she might change her mind about me. And then there'd be the whole week apart from each other. That could distance us even more. I couldn't bear these thoughts. A part of me knew they were stupid, and that Antonia would never be so shallow, but another part was getting all churned up.

After breakfast Antonia wanted to phone her parents, so I decided to phone Mum at the same time.

It felt great telling her about my new best friend, and as I talked I gradually stopped worrying about the differences between Antonia and me, although when the words "best friend" first popped out of my mouth it gave me a bit of a jolt, because in actual fact, Antonia and I had never discussed whether or not we were *best* friends and she might not feel as I did about that. All she'd said was *amiche* – friends. I loved that word, and I thought I was quite good at pronouncing it now.

Mum sounded really happy to hear my news, and asked if there was any particular reason why Antonia and I had suddenly got close to each other, as we'd been in the same dorm for a whole fortnight, yet I'd never mentioned her after the first day. I said it was just that it had taken us a while to get to know each other. Then I explained that she was Italian, and that she was quite homesick, missing her family when they were so far away.

"Aah, poor thing," said Mum in a sympathetic

voice. "Well, it's nice that she's got you, sweetheart." Her voice suddenly brightened right up. "Maybe, once she's more used to the school and not feeling so homesick, she'd like to come and spend a few days with us at home in one of the holidays?"

"Y...yes," I said, hesitantly. "I'm sure she'd love to." But another cloud went scudding across my sunny blue sky at the thought of taking Antonia in the back of our old Volvo to our little terraced house.

Almost as though Mum could sense what I was thinking, she suddenly came out with something incredible that cheered me right up. "Oh, guess what, sweetheart?"

"What?"

"I've got myself a little runaround – a Mini Cooper!"

"Hey, that's cool!" I said. "So you can come and collect me in it, can't you?"

"Well, it's only a little car and I know the girls are desperate to come along too, and with your bags and stuff, it might be easier to come in Dad's car."

My heart sank. It would have been great if Mum had picked me up in her car – then I wouldn't have to worry about the paints and things in the back of Dad's old Volvo.

* * *

I was so happy with my life at Silver Spires now that Antonia and I had sorted all our problems out. Every day, we seemed to recall another time when one of us had been upset by the other one, and it was really sweet because Antonia always insisted we clamber up onto one or other of our beds and have another "truth talk". The others agreed with me that the name "truth talk" was really sweet, and Sasha said it would be good if we made a kind of rule that if ever anyone needed a heart-to-heart discussion, they could call a truth talk and we would all squash onto that person's bed. The number of times we all six sat on Antonia's or my bed was amazing. One of us would bring up something that had happened, then we went through a big explanation about it, and always finished up smiling at how we'd managed to get things so wrong. Apparently, the time when her eyes had looked so fiery as she'd shut her wardrobe door and said it was too late to see her dress, it was because she could tell I was upset at seeing Sasha's and Izzy's party clothes and she didn't want to make me feel worse. And when she'd eyed my old woolly bag on the way to the minibus that time, she was dying to tell me how much she loved the bag, but didn't dare in case it came out sounding wrong. Poor Antonia.

The two of us made sure we spent as much time as possible together, and in our free moments we often went to the library, where I tried to help her with her English and her schoolwork in general. One day she told me excitedly that the maths and science teachers had both said she was going up a set after half-term and that if she carried on like this she'd be going up again after Christmas. I felt so happy when I heard that.

French was Antonia's best subject, because she said it was very similar to Italian in many ways, so when we had French prep it was often Antonia helping *me*. It was lovely being able to sit next to her for everything except English, maths and science, and I couldn't wait till we'd be together for those subjects too. Even after school we stuck together, both going to the same clubs – we'd compromised on fashion and debating society, because Antonia insisted that her English would improve if she had to discuss things. And at weekends, we always went on the same outings.

The house staff found us quite amusing, I think, but I could tell they liked the way we were such good friends now, because we always got special smiles from them. Matron had started a competition between herself and me to see who could learn the most Italian words before the half-term holiday, and when there was only one day to go we compared notes, and it turned out that I knew far more than her. I did admit that I had an unfair advantage because I saw Antonia so much more than she did, and Matron said that was true, and that I'd better watch out, because she was going to study like mad over half-term and give us both a big surprise when we came back to Silver Spires.

The final day before the holiday was a Saturday, and all us girls were due to be picked up by our parents or guardians after lunch, any time between two and five o'clock. We were allowed to leave as much stuff as we wanted in our dorms over the half-term break, because there would always be someone here and the dorms would be locked. We didn't have lessons on Saturday morning so we could sort out and pack all our stuff, and have a nice time with our friends.

Emerald dorm looked a right tip throughout the whole morning, as we all kept changing our minds about how much stuff to take home with us. Antonia didn't pack much at all, because she said she had tons more clothes at home. Now that I understand the way Antonia is, I realize she's not showing off or anything when she talks like that. She's just stating a fact. I planned to leave one of my bags in the basement and quite a bit of my stuff here in the dorm, but to take my other bag home.

I'd thought and thought about the car situation, and I knew I'd so much prefer it if Mum and my sisters came to pick me up in the Mini Cooper. I felt really guilty and horrible, but I phoned Dad in a last attempt to try to get him to change his mind about coming to collect me.

"There's no need for you to take a day off work, Dad, honestly," I said in my lightest tone.

"Don't you worry yourself about that, Nicole. I worked the last two Saturdays, so I deserve this weekend off!" Then his voice quietened. "And don't worry that your mum and I will argue…"

"No, it's okay." Poor Dad sounded quite embarrassed, and obviously thought that I was trying to put him off coming because of the way he and Mum had argued when they'd brought me here on the first day. I'd actually forgotten about those angry words that had passed between them though, because my mind had been so full of worries about how old the car was, and how messy, and what on earth I would say to explain so many paint cans still being in there.

By the end of the phone call with Dad, I felt totally wound up, because not only was he definitely coming in the Volvo with Mum and Clare and Clemmie, but to make matters worse, he was planning on arriving at the beginning of the afternoon, which meant that all my friends would still be there to see them.

At two o'clock on the dot, us six from Emerald dorm gathered in the hall of Forest Ash and kept on looking out of the window to see if any cars were arriving.

"What make is your car, Nicole?" asked Sasha.

"It's…a Volvo."

"What colour?" Izzy wanted to know.

"Blue," replied Antonia.

My heart hammered. She was so observant.

"We will talk online every day, yes?" she went on, even though we'd already promised and promised to do that.

"Yes," I laughed, happily. "Every day."

The others were just having the same kind of conversation amongst themselves, when Antonia suddenly said, "They are here! I see the car!"

And she was right. Our old car was slowly pulling into the drive outside Forest Ash. I swallowed and tried not to go red.

"I do not want you to go!" said Antonia.

I gave her a big hug, then we all went outside just as Mum was getting out of the passenger seat. She didn't spot me at first.

"Your mother's really pretty," said Sasha in a whisper.

I'd never actually thought about whether Mum was pretty or not, so that gave me a surprise. Then Clare and Clemmie were scrambling out of the back and Clemmie spotted me straight away. "Nicole!" she called out, rushing over and flinging herself at me. "I've been dying for this moment!"

I bent down to hug her but she kept her arms wound round my neck so I couldn't straighten up.

"Ah! Sweet!" I heard Izzy say.

Then Clare wanted a hug too, and it was only when I'd introduced both my sisters to all my friends at top speed that I looked at Mum and Dad and noticed something different about them, but I couldn't work out what it was. They were standing by the car as though waiting their turn for a hug. I hurried over to them and they both came towards me at the same moment, so it was like a triple hug, as I used to call them when I was little.

And that was when it hit me. Mum and Dad didn't seem to mind about being so close to each other now, whereas the last time I'd seen them together they were all spiky and distant with one another.

Mum was smiling like mad and I realized that Sasha was right. She was really pretty. I took her hand and led her towards my friends.

"This is, Antonia, Mum."

"I am very pleased to meet you, Mrs. Weelliamson," said Antonia in her politest voice. "You have a very clever and very kind daughter!"

Mum burst into laughter, then suddenly her eyes were bright with tears. "I know, Antonia, but thank you for saying it. And I think Nicole's lucky to have such a lovely friend."

"This is my dad, Antonia."

Dad shook hands with her, then looked a bit embarrassed. "Sorry, bit dirty…" he mumbled.

"That's 'cos Daddy's painted the whole house, Nicole!" said Clemmie, all wide-eyed, as though she loved being the one to tell me the news.

"At long last!" said Mum, grinning round at my friends. "We're always last in line, I'm afraid."

Sasha and the others laughed politely, but I saw Antonia frowning and realized she didn't understand what Mum meant. And in that instant I knew I had two choices. I could change the subject so Antonia would never know what Mum meant about Dad only painting our house when he'd finished painting everyone else's houses. *Or* I could explain exactly what Mum meant, so Antonia knew the whole truth.

I didn't hesitate for one moment, and it wasn't just because of wanting Antonia to know the truth. It was because something had happened inside me. I was suddenly filled with pride for my family, and with something else too. I think it was confidence, but whatever it was, I knew for sure that I had absolutely nothing to be ashamed of. My words came out strongly, even though I was still a teeny bit shaky inside. I just needed to get to the end of my sentence and check that the look in Antonia's eyes hadn't changed.

"Dad's job is painting other people's houses, and Mum meant that we had to wait in a line until Dad had time to paint our own house."

Antonia broke into a beaming smile. "Wait een *una fila*!" she said proudly. "Yes, I understand!" Then she turned to Mum. "Thees ees what my mother says about my father when she wants heem to cook!"

Mum laughed. "Oh, your dad's a chef! Lucky you!"

Then Clemmie was tugging on my hand. "I want to see where you sleep!" she said.

So we all made our way into Forest Ash, and while Mum and Dad stayed in the hall to have a chat with Mrs. Pridham, the rest of us went up to Emerald, Clemmie and Clare running on ahead and calling out, "Tell us when to stop!"

"Top floor!" I shouted.

"Your parents are really cool!" said Izzy.

"And just like *my* parents," said Antonia.

I turned my head sharply to see what Antonia meant, because surely my parents had absolutely nothing in common with hers.

"Yes, they are very...how would I say eet in Engleesh? Er...very close," she said. "Yes, very close."

I knew I was staring at her as though she was speaking Italian and I couldn't understand a word. "You...you think so?"

"Yes, I *know* so."

I turned and leaned over the banister of the first-floor landing. Mum and Dad were right next to each other as they talked to Mrs. Pridham, and Mum was smiling up at Dad.

"Oh...yes!" I said slowly. And I felt a lovely shimmer of happiness that my parents were getting on so well with each other.

Antonia laughed, then grabbed both my hands. "Are you excited to think of seeing your house all painted?" she asked me happily.

I nodded. "I'm really looking forward to the whole week," I told her. "But I'm also looking forward to coming back here. Aren't you?"

She nodded hard. "I weell be sad to leave my family again. But thees time I weell have my new friend!"

"Yes," I said simply. "You will."

"Look! The sun has come out!" said Antonia. "Let us see the spires before you go."

So we called to the others that we'd see them outside, and Clemmie called back that it was okay because Izzy was looking after them. Then we went out together, past our old Volvo, that had caused me so much worry and yet didn't bother me in the slightest any more now that I realized I'd truly got the nicest friends in the world, who would never dream of not liking a person just because they came from a different background.

And as we walked towards the main building, I was still thinking how stupid I'd been to get myself into such a state about everything, when Antonia

148

stopped my thoughts by gripping my hand as she looked up. "There!" she breathed. "What does eet remind you of?"

"Diamonds," I said quietly, as I stared up at the sparkling silver spires.

"Diamonds, yes." Then she looked at me with her big dark eyes. "I knew we would be *amiche del cuore* from the moment you said that word all that long time ago. "

"What's *amiche del cuore*?" I asked.

"I think you say...*best* friends?" she said, a question mark in her voice.

"Yes, we do!" I said with a catch in my voice. "That's exactly what we say!"

Nicole's Top Ten Party Tips

I loved our party at Silver Spires – and now it's your turn to celebrate! Here are my top ten tips for perfect party fun...

★ Send out invitations early. You could even design your own e-vites for that personal touch.

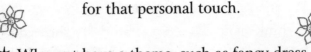

★ Why not have a theme, such as fancy dress or a makeover night? Or if your birthday's around Hallowe'en, what about a spookfest?

★ Try party picnics in the summer, or even a camp-out sleepover in your back garden...

★ Why not share your party with a best friend? It's half the work and twice the fun!

★ On party day, get your friends to help decorate and set up. It'll make things less stressful for you, plus you're bound to have so much fun together it'll feel like the party's already started!

★ Don't panic about what to wear – just make
sure you feel comfortable, and always add
a little party sparkle!

★ Use paper plates and cups to save
on washing-up…but remember to recycle
them afterwards!

★ Keep your snacks simple – fun finger food like
pizza slices, veggie bites with dips, and brownies all
work well. Plus why not make fairy cakes and then
put out lots of fun toppings for your guests
to decorate them with?

★ Once the party's in full swing, don't worry
if there's a hiccup with some of your plans…
no one knows what you were planning anyway!

**So what are you waiting for? Grab your
friends and have some School Friends fun!**

Nicole

Now read on for a sneak preview of

Dancer at Silver Spires

I stared around the dining hall and thought for at least the hundredth time how much I love it here at Silver Spires. I suppose all boarding schools are great, but I just don't see how they can be as great as this one. I mean, I was so nervous when I started here eight weeks ago, but the very first time I came into this dining hall with the other five girls from my dormitory, I felt so happy. It was obvious we were going to get on with each other. Well, it's true I did feel a bit anxious about Antonia, who's Italian, and Nicole, who's amazingly clever. Those two didn't seem to hit it off as well as the rest of us, but

I felt sure it would work out eventually because they both seemed so nice. And I was right. They're best friends now.

My own best friend is called Sasha, and while I was staring around right then, she was listening intently to something that Emily was telling her. Even though Emily's story seemed to be going on and on, and personally I tuned out ages before, Sasha still looked interested. She kept nodding slowly, her big blue eyes looking straight at Emily. And that's because Sasha is such a fantastic listener. I'm so glad we're best friends.

As soon as lunch was over we all set off through the grounds for afternoon lessons. It was maths first, and that's one of the three subjects we've been put in sets for, which means that we six friends aren't all together for those lessons, like we are for everything else.

"See you later!" called Antonia, as she went off with Emily and Emily's best friend, Bryony.

"I can't believe how good Antonia's getting at English!" said Sasha. "And her English accent's getting better too."

"I know!" said Nicole, looking happy. "And it's great that she's been put up a set for maths and science."

I nodded. "If she carries on going up, you two might be together in top sets for everything before the end of Year Seven!"

Nicole laughed. "That would be really good," she said, linking arms with me on one side and Sasha on the other and falling into step with us. But almost immediately she pulled away, half laughing. "Do you know, I always feel a bit like an elephant when I'm walking beside you, Izzy!"

Sasha laughed too. "I know exactly what you mean!"

My body slumped instinctively as the little voice in my head started up. *Not this again*.

Nicole must have sensed my dejection. "Oh, Izzy, it's a compliment, you know," she said. "You're just so graceful."

Sasha grinned at me. "Except when you deliberately don't stand up straight, like right now."

"I'd love to have great posture, like you," Nicole added.

I tried to smile while my mind searched around for a quick way of getting off this terrible subject, and the voice in my head grew louder. *I don't want to talk about being graceful and standing up straight. I don't even want to think about it. I know where it leads.*

"You'd make a great dancer, Izzy," said Sasha.

I didn't reply because I couldn't think of what to say. We'd had this kind of conversation lots of times since I'd started at Silver Spires and no one knew how much I hated it. Well, actually that's not true. I thought Sasha was starting to notice how uncomfortable I got whenever anyone mentioned me in the same breath as dancing or ballet, and how I always tried to quickly change the conversation. The trouble is, Sasha's such a good listener that I'm afraid one of these days I might be tempted to tell her about my past. But it's a secret. If I told her about the *other me*, she'd think I was completely mad.

And just when I was thinking about my past an annoying voice popped into my head. *Is it that she'll think you're mad, or just that you can't ever let yourself talk about it?*

Suddenly I felt shaky. The truth had finally hit me.

It's not that I won't talk about it, it's that I *can't*.

To find out what happens next, read

 Dancer at Silver Spires

Complete your

School Friends

collection!

Party at Silver Spires
ISBN 9780746098646
Nicole's determined to keep her scholarship a secret, in case it stops her from making friends with her dorm.

Dancer at Silver Spires
ISBN 9780746098653
Izzy's trying to put her hopes of becoming a ballerina behind her – until the school puts on a dance show.

Dreams at Silver Spires
ISBN 9780746098660
Emily dreams of starting a cool club at school...but first she must persuade the teachers she's got what it takes.

Magic at Silver Spires
ISBN 9780746098677
Antonia and her friends must prove to her parents that she belongs at Silver Spires...before they take her back to Italy!

Success at Silver Spires
ISBN 9780746098684
Sasha is delighted when she discovers her natural talent for sports, but she faces tough competition from a rival.

Mystery at Silver Spires
ISBN 9780746098691
Bryony keeps hearing spooky noises in the night. Is the school haunted, or has the dorm got an unexpected guest?

About the Author

Ann Bryant's School Days

Who was your favourite teacher?
At primary it was Mr. Perks – we called him Perksy. I was in his class in Year Six, and most days he let me work on a play I was writing! At secondary, my fave teacher was Mrs. Rowe, simply because I loved her subject (French) and she was so young and pretty and slim and chic and it was great seeing what new clothes she'd be wearing.

What were your best and worst lessons?
My brain doesn't process history, geography or science and I hated cookery, so those were my least favourite subjects. But I was good at English, music, French and PE, so I loved those. I also enjoyed art, although I was completely rubbish at it!

What was your school uniform like?
We had to wear a white shirt with a navy blue tie and sweater, and a navy skirt, but there was actually a wide variety of styles allowed – I was a very small

person and liked pencil-thin skirts. We all rolled them over and over at the waist!

Did you take part in after-school activities?
Well I loved just hanging out with my friends, but most of all I loved ballet and went to extra classes in Manchester after school.

Did you have any pets while you were at school?
My parents weren't animal lovers so we were only allowed a goldfish! But since I had my two daughters, we've had loads – two cats, two guinea pigs, two rabbits, two hamsters and two goldfish.

What was your most embarrassing moment?
When I was in Year Seven I had to play piano for assembly. It was April Fool's Day and the piano wouldn't work (it turned out that someone had put a book in the back). I couldn't bring myself to stand up and investigate because that would draw attention to me, so I sat there with my hands on the keys wishing to die, until the Deputy Head came and rescued me!

To find out more about Ann Bryant visit her website: www.annbryant.co.uk

Want to know more about the
Silver Spires girls?

Or try a quiz to discover which
School Friend you're most like?

You can even send Silver Spires e-cards
to your best friends and post your own
book reviews online!

It's all at

www.silverspiresschool.co.uk

Check it out now!